You need confidence before you walk down Yellow Street with a big fat wad a green. Yeah, its morning but lots a business goes down in the morning on Yellow Street. Junkies still wandering for a fix and hos that didnt make enough for their pimps. Us three are pretty hardcore for kids but it aint like none of us are packing chrome.

We arent even off the stoop before Midge kneels down and investigates our jackolantern like shes from CSI Miami. Must be some beetles or worms up inside that big orange bitch. Moms bought it from some banger with a shopping cart full a pumpkins and even though it was fungused I was psyched cuz Moms hardly ever gets out of bed and when she does its only to cross the street to reup her cigs cuz the dude that works there wont let me buy any for her. Last time Moms acquired me something special like that was once upon a time and a galaxy far away.

Here its Halloween day and the jackolanterns mouth is sucked in like No Teeth Mike, this dude that shoots up across from school. Its all withered and rotten and a gross poop color. Every time I look at it I think about Moms cuz shes the one that bought it special for me and also cuz shes up in her room getting all withered and rotten too. [illegible]ybe Moms has bugs in her head like the jackolantern [illegible] That would explain a lot.

Theres a Christmas tree [illegible] got a gummy price tag and [illegible] Christmas? Nope. Christmas [illegible] gonna be Halloween forever…

ALSO BY DANIEL KRAUS:

THE SHAPE OF WATER *(with Guillermo del Toro)*
THE DEATH AND LIFE OF ZEBULON FINCH
Volume One: At the Edge of Empire
Volume Two: Empire Decayed
TROLLHUNTERS *(with Guillermo del Toro)*
SCOWLER
ROTTERS
THE MONSTER VARIATIONS

SOME OTHER HARD CASE CRIME BOOKS YOU WILL ENJOY:

JOYLAND *by Stephen King*
THE COCKTAIL WAITRESS *by James M. Cain*
BRAINQUAKE *by Samuel Fuller*
THIEVES FALL OUT *by Gore Vidal*
SO NUDE, SO DEAD *by Ed McBain*
THE GIRL WITH THE DEEP BLUE EYES
by Lawrence Block
QUARRY *by Max Allan Collins*
BUST *by Ken Bruen and Jason Starr*
SOHO SINS *by Richard Vine*
THE KNIFE SLIPPED *by Erle Stanley Gardner*
SNATCH *by Gregory Mcdonald*
THE LAST STAND *by Mickey Spillane*
UNDERSTUDY FOR DEATH *by Charles Willeford*
CHARLESGATE CONFIDENTIAL *by Scott Von Doviak*
SO MANY DOORS *by Oakley Hall*
BROTHERS KEEPERS *by Donald E. Westlake*
A BLOODY BUSINESS *by Dylan Struzan*
THE TRIUMPH OF THE SPIDER MONKEY
by Joyce Carol Oates

Blood SUGAR

by **Daniel Kraus**

CRIME NOVEL

A HARD CASE CRIME BOOK
(HCC-141)
First Hard Case Crime edition: October 2019

Published by

Titan Books
A division of Titan Publishing Group Ltd
144 Southwark Street
London SE1 0UP

in collaboration with Winterfall LLC

Print edition ISBN 978-1-78909-193-9
E-book ISBN 978-1-78909-194-6

Design direction by Max Phillips
www.signalfoundry.com

Typeset by Swordsmith Productions

Printed in the United States of America

Visit us on the web at www.HardCaseCrime.com

for Jason Davis
& Simone Lueck

A foraging wild creature, intent above all upon survival, is as strong as the grass.

—Richard Adams, *Watership Down*

BLOOD SUGAR

Money

Fat boy says hes gonna put crack inside Fun Size Snickers. I guess he went ahead and lost his dang mind. News flash, Robbie, crack is rocks, and you cant squoosh rocks inside Fun Size Snickers without ruining the Fun Size shape. Thats some idiotical sharkweek right there so I go <Im jonesing, man, Im jonesing, how about you hook a little man up with some sweet supermilk instead?> Robbie doesnt smile or nothing. Dudes trying to be some kind of hard ass robocop. Says no poopypants baby that still skid marks his drawers oughta joke out loud about a grown mans personal stash.

The mightyduck is he grumping for? The chunky butts seen me hit a whole thing a Reddi Whip till I got crunk. Saw me get torched on a big bowl a dank too. Dang, I puked a whole bottle a stank ass apricot schnapps while he just sat there and laughed his fat ass off. I dont say none a that out loud though cuz what if Robbie thinks all that stuff is poopypants baby stuff? One thing I dont need is more teasing from Robbie cuz when he teases he does it real hurtful.

So I switch up my play and go <Be cool, Robbie, its no thing> and then fat boys all smiles. He calls me by my actual real name, Jody, which he hardly dont ever do, and he says <Im glad to hear that Jody cuz I need you to go fetch me some

candies, so are you gonna stand there holding your dick all morning or are you gonna walk your pale pasty ass down to Walgreen for some Fun Size Snickers like I said?>

Walgreen can suck my left ball. Target is my preferential shopping experience by far. But the truth is, Walgreen is the only place even close to Robbies crib that sells stuff. I get dogging Robbie hard about how I dont want to go down there cuz its cold and mean old Dick Trickle works there but Robbie straight up ignores my ass. What he starts doing is chinups on this stupid chinup bar he wedged in the doorway. Guess where the mightyducker bought that cheap piece a junk? Walgreen!

Anyway it looks funny cuz Robbies this big fat dude that cant do two chins without a heart attack. Hes got all this pussy ass black hair down his neck plus pimples all across his flab cheeks and the saddest little mustache you ever saw. When fat boy pounds out his chins, all two a them, you can peep his whole big white blubber belly. I get a laugh out of that cuz my own abs are tight, even if Im mad short. Dag always looks away like looking aint polite. Dag is wrong about that though cuz that mightyducking sharkweek is hilarious as sharkweek!

In case youre wondering why I cuss so polite let me explain. Robbie doesnt stand for cussing no more since he broke up with Little Lamb. Last time I cussed normal Robbie grabbed my shirt and said no little man like me oughta run his mouth like that cuz it dont show respect for your elders or even your dang self, and I said well what am I supposed to say then, and he said how is he supposed to know, so I just took the titles of interesting programs I saw on Moms TV.

Robbie bails out on his chins. Dudes old as hell, about thirty is what Dag says, and after he mops up his old man sweat and makes sure his heart didnt explode, he points at me and Dag and Midget like hes Tom Cruise and we are the Mission Impossibles. He says he dont trust my ass at Walgreen, not with his money he dont, so he wants the girlies to come with. Thats humorous cuz Dags ten times the klepto I am. Normally Id a been like, yo, how about you roll your own obese ass to Walgreen? Except fat boy said his money. Fat ass is handing over his own money to buy candy. Thats some unprecedented sharkweek right there.

Also I guess I should be honest and tell you Ive got pinkeye for the third time this year so it could be Robbie doesnt want to hand me the money direct from his hand and if thats the case I cant really blame him. Pinkeyes contagious as hell.

Course Dag gets dubious like she does and asks how come hes sending three kids? Dang, girl, I know the answer to that! Walgreen caught Robbie lifting a Gillette Mach 5 three months back and now they keep a video cam snap of Robbie taped on the register. But Dag is Dag and she goes on all opinionated about how Robbie doesnt have any excuse to stay home cuz its not like hes wheelchair fat. Ha! Robbie gives her a look like hes King Théoden from Two Towers and he sits his royal butt down on his busted ass easy chair that has a Dominos box to cushion his sore back. Fat boys backs always paining him. Then he lays his whole plan out. I end up super glad Dag asked cuz what Robbie says is straight up nuts.

Basically Robbie explains how hes gonna put all kinds a hard ass drugs into normal ass candies and pass that stuff out to trick or treaters tonight. See, this is why I hang out with this fat fool. Robbies dull as a park bench most days but every once in a while, blam, he does something crazy nobody ever ever saw coming. Like the time he bought himself two tarantulas, they were like tarantula brother and sister I guess, and he let them crawl their hairy asses all around the crib. Course then fat boy couldnt get neither one from under the couch and suddenly got all super scared of tarantulas and all a us were hopping on top the furniture and screaming, and when Robbie finally scooted them in a bucket he went straight out back and filled that bucket with dirt and buried that bucket and since then no ones ever mentioned nothing about any tarantulas.

This candy plan is double or triple times more messed up than anything Robbies ever planned. Dag acts like she already knows about it. She tells Robbie to tell me how come hes gonna do it, and Robbie is like them assheads deserve it, and Dag says to explain how children can be assheads if their brains arent grown, and Robbie says hes talking about their asshead parents. Dag looks at me and

Midge and nods wise cuz like <See?> And we all feel that truth. Grown up adults have been doing Robbie wrong since forever and I guess they probably are due for revenge.

Sounds like a lot of work though so Im like nah lets chill and wait for Ellen to come on cuz that dyke is amusing as hell. Its eight in the dang morning, right? So I put my feet up on the TV and thats when sharkweek gets real. Robbie shakes like hes having the DTs and his eyes go all watery and when it comes to Robbie watery eyes dont indicate being sad, it indicates total ninja rage. Fat boys so large, if he lays into you he can break a bone. So I take my feet down and I go <Chill, man, Ill get you your candies!> Its not like Im shook for real or nothing but dang. I dont need another broke toe. Broke toes take forever to heal and they make you run like a bitch.

Midgets so excited about getting candies she might tinkle her drawers. Little sister is psycho for sugar. Course theres no way youd know that cuz Midget doesnt talk, but shes been my foster sister over a year now so Ive had plenty a time to do scientific observation. Sister eats sugar straight outta the dang packet. One time ants were in the sugar and Midget didnt give a mightyduck! Crazy little ho went crazy on that stuff. When she finished there was one little black ant dude fighting to crawl out her mouth. Serious, yo, I was rooting for that little guy but nope. He got slurped.

Supermilk

Robbie gives Dag a big fat roll a cash. Kinda burns me up to be honest. Just cuz Dag lives in Pinebluff Glenn Estates, fat boy thinks shes more responsible than me? If shes so responsible, how come she spends so much time on Yellow Street in Robbies craphole? If anyones in charge of us three kids its me. Dags been following me around since she started public school. Yeah, I know. It sounds like she wants my wiener. She dont though. Cant blame her either. Like I said, Im mad short.

School was where me and Dag first met up. Recess, three years back. Guess you could say it was fateful and whatnot. She rolled up while I was trying to crack open the ribs a this bird. You know, for science. I mean, the bird was dead. Aint like he was pecking me. But Dag rolls up and starts bugging cuz she says Ill catch bacterial plague. So I dig around till I find this DVD in the gutter called Hope Floats and I start using that instead a my hands but Dag doesnt approve a that either cuz she says Sandra Bullocks is a Oscar winning actress and you have to respect that. I was like, bitch, Sandra Bullocks aint ever won a dang Oscar! And she starts talking Oscars like shes a professor of Oscar studies. Godfather Two and Ben Hur and Rain Man, all kinds a crazy sharkweek.

Im not even gonna front. Shorty schooled me serious, so when the recess bell ringed I asked if she enjoyed cool junk cuz I knew this dude Robbie that has a place thats like the

Minas Tirith of junk and if she wanted we could go there after school. Then I had to educate her what Minas Tirith is. Girlfriend hadnt ever seen Lord of the Rings! Knew five million fun facts about Sandra Bullocks but not a single thing about Hobbiton or Mordor. Im telling you I about pooped my pants. She came over and thats how I started knowing Dag and how she lives in Pinebluff Glenn Estates and has two good parents and a sister called Lotte in the nuthouse.

Thats how me and Dag, and then Midget once Moms fostered her ass, how we got hanging together the three of us with Robbie. Cribs stank as hell but I didnt lie about the junk. Best rusted ass crap you ever seen. The front yards got a go cart skeleton and a big huge engine from I dont even know. Airplane, maybe? Midget can squeeze her whole body inside it and take a nap. Backyards even better. Theres a semi cab back there and old fridges and fascinating motorcycle wheels and a million bed springs that make a rust storm every time the wind kicks up.

When Robbie gets feeling low he goes on about how it didnt used to be junk. He says back when he lived here with his real biological family all the junk was work his dad was doing for pay. I guess his dad had wizard skills at fixing objects. Robbie says everything was shiny and amazing. Me, I prefer like it is now. You could build yourself a Peter Jackson castle out a all that junk with walls so high nobody could ever do evil to you or drag your butt to school or nothing. Walls like that, you could protect your family. Even if your fam is just three half ass kids with nowhere better else to go.

I dont have the personal muscle tone to push all that junk around myself. Too dang skinny, cant lift for sharkweek even though, for real, my abs are tight.

Its not that we aint psyched to have fat boys cash, its just weird, right? So while Dags doing her hair up and Midgets doing a tinkle I take a sec to glop the cheese outta my pinkeye and ask Robbie what drugs hes got on hand to put inside the candies cuz I aint seen him use in forever. Fat boy scratches his greasy hair like a dog and wipes the grease across all ten thousand a his pimples.

Robbie goofs up a grin and says <Dont worry about it, little man, I have a brand new hookup.>

That dont set me at ease zero. I remember fat boys last hookup and that ended poor. Robbie got late with the chip and got beat down hard. His ear bled for a hour and his eyebrow flopped down like a fake mustache. Dag goobed iodine or peroxide or some kind a medical liquid on it while Robbie cried how he wasnt gonna ever use again, how he was gonna go cold turkey, all that. Dag didnt question none a that sharkweek. She just fixed his mangled face clean as a doctor. Made me proud as hell.

Now its like Robbies forgot his own personal history. He tells me how hes gonna call his new dealer man while we do Walgreen and how hes gonna order up a big package but I say <Why dont you do it right now, mister chicken man?> Sometimes Im dumb as hell. Robbie leaps up all dramatic and chucks a Us Weekly at me and after he misses he starts chucking heavier items that used to belong to his pops like the stapler and the stool and the Seinfeld mug. I bob and weave like UFC. Nobodys got the skills to slow down my evasive action!

Whole things pretty enjoyable till a hand exerciser hits Dag while shes beautying her hair and she whips around cold as ice. Dag dont have to say a word when shes pissed. Robbie hangs his head down shameful and looks at his pops broken old Seinfeld mug. He looks at it like its meaningful and the big new crack in it is meaningful too. He sits in his Dominos box chair and apologizes real sensitive.

He goes <I really regret my actions, Dagmar.> When Dag puts her hand on her hip all doubtful he goes <Of course Id never want to accidentally hurt you or Midget, you both mean so much to me.> When Dag crosses her arms like shes skeptical Robbie goes so low its nothing but whispers. <Wont you please forgive me?> Thing is, with Robbies greasy ass hair and crusty ass pimples and sad ass face, dang. Even I feel bad for the man. We three are the only people fat boys got.

Dag sighs like whatever, but its enough to get Robbie puppy dogging. He jumps up and claps his hands and says how about he fixes us supermilks when we get back? Just like that the whole mood a the day changes.

Supermilks the bomb. Robbie used to have a wonderful job holding road signs that told folks to drive slow cuz a construction and it was lucrative as hell. Back then he fixed us supermilks all the dang time. Now theyre rarer than gold. Mostly only Christmas and birthdays and Easters and whatnot. St Patrick too cuz Robbie claims hes Irish, the great great great great great grandson of an Irish king and one day hes gonna inherit an actual real ass castle with a real ass moat thatll protect all our royal asses. I doubt it but who knows. Robbies full a mystery.

The recipe for supermilk is first you take whatever streetready junk you got lying around. Doesnt matter if its blow or ice or X or H or K or any a those alphabeticals cuz theyre all getting blended up in the blender. Next you pour in some sugar, and malt if you got it, and definitely plenty a milk cuz growing children need milk for powerful bones. When its blended real smooth you serve it up in special frosty glasses you frosted in the freezer. Then guess what? Then you get crunk!

Supermilks cold and creamy and also a fun surprise cuz you never know how its gonna play. Best trip I ever had was this time everything in the crib went real pale, the yellow stains on the ceiling and the mice turds in the carpet, all a it paling real bright like the world was a plastic bag and I was seeing right through it. Once for like an experiment Dag gulped her supermilk real fast and kept saying how her heart ached and we laughed cuz it was a funny thing to say but it was true cuz I felt it myself, real careful so I didnt touch her titties, and her heart was like it was trying to break her dang ribs.

For Midget, the time I think about most was when she seizured and supermilk came out her mouth looking like cool whip and me and Robbie got afraid and put little sister in cold bathtub water even though Dag kept giggling. When Midge woke up she licked it off her paws cuz I guess she thought it looked like cool whip too and you know how shes psycho for sugar. I laughed but Robbie didnt. He looked serious as a easter island head, like all the people he ever cared about just kicked the big old bucket.

To Whom It May Concern:

That's how Mr. Toppen told us to begin a letter if you didn't know who to write it to exactly & I don't know who to write it to exactly bc I'm writing to both of you equally. If you're confused Mom & Dad this is your son Robbie & you might say How Is That Possible bc how did Robbie who we LEFT BEHIND get our address to write us but it was easy. You always underestimate me bc I did poorly in school & then got involved in Violence but I'm not really very dumb.

All I had to do was call Uncle Gary & at first he said ~~piss off~~ go away & I shouldn't call you Mom & Dad & he cried bc I bet he was picturing Mom as his little sis back in the day but I was Very Firm & I told him I'm their son who Mom & Dad LEFT BEHIND & I had a Legal Right so he gave me your current address & said God forgive me & please do not visit Mom & Dad in person. That part made me mad bc I wouldn't do that to Mom who hates big scenes & I've already embarrassed both of you so much since all the Violence.

Don't panic Mom & Dad although I was LEFT BEHIND all I want to tell you is I'm taking good care of the house after you left Very Quickly without warning me at all. Your #1 concern is probably How Can Dumb Robbie Pay The Bills but I'll have you know Mr. Toppen taught us how to do bills bc some kids had Drunks & Druggies for parents & so bc of that lesson I paid some bills with No Problem although now I have to stop bc I went ~~ass up~~ bankrupt which brings me to Money & how I don't have any left.

Don't worry about Money too much Mom & Dad bc when I got LEFT BEHIND you didn't take hardly any of your stuff including all the junk Dad was repairing & I know Dad I should phrase it Pieces all the Pieces you LEFT BEHIND just like me. I don't know as much about fixing Pieces as you Dad with your Mechanical Genius but I've hit the books & you might be Proud of the work I did on Mr. Fielder's Harley Davidson carburetor although to be Totally Honest I did burn the fuel tank to a crisp & Mr. Fielder was ~~pissed~~ unsatisfied & threw a bowling ball through the kitchen window which would have been Very Bad except the window was already gone & it just ripped the middle out of a plastic bag.

My plan is to gain pro skills at fixing Pieces & earn Decent Money & build a giant Quonset Hut for the Pieces so they aren't willy nilly over the yard bc Mom thought that was trashy & I agree & then use the Net Profits to build an 18x40x54 above ground pool bc I think when people hear about how I have a top quality above ground pool complete with decking & landscaping they'll want to swim in it & they'll see how Normal I am & not Violent & I think many people who don't like me will become friends & some of them close personal friends. It's a solid long term business plan but for now it would be best if you sent Money for Bills as fast as possible. I am ~~up shit creek~~ ~~screwed~~ in a bind.

There is also the Lawsuit. It is a depressing thing to talk about between parents & their only son after the inspiring discussion of the above ground pool but I know you know about the Lawsuit bc I was a Minor at the time of the Incident & you had to sign Documents & Letters & Affidavits & Testimony. A clerk said I was being assigned a lawyer named Mr. Mantle but if Mr. Mantle is a Big Shot like OJ had I'd rather have a ~~cheap ass~~ reasonably priced lawyer to save you money Mom & Dad. Honestly my concern about Money has made me sick on the toilet & so I'm being Up Front about it & sharing it with you. You know the address where to send Money bc you used to live here.

In the meantime I promise on Gramma's grave to keep things nice. I know Mom you were Very Proud of your 10 piece Ginsu Gourmet Cutlery Set so I won't use them except on big thick steaks so they stay Very Sharp. I know Dad you didn't leave your Seinfeld mug behind on purpose so I'll only use it when all other mugs are totally disgusting. Most of all I'll keep the Clocks which are Important Heirlooms in top notch working condition. I have hit the books on clocks & know the difference between Grandfather & Cuckoo & Pendulum & Atomic & Mechanical & Electric & Quartz & Countdown & Flip & Lantern & Lighthouse. I hope you're impressed Dad bc to be honest I'm trying to impress you.

I admit I'm currently doing a ~~piss poor~~ not great job at winding the clocks & pulling the chains. You probably know I missed my first Court Date with Mr. Mantle bc I got messed up by the clocks. The Judge was Very Upset & that mistake is On Me! Although Mom & Dad I think Total Honesty will create a superior relationship for us & so I'll tell you I was Using at the time & would've slept through the clocks anyway. Mom please don't cry I know Using is Very Bad but it helps with my headaches & I know people don't believe me bc of my Stupid History but the headaches are terrible & sometimes I can't see & can't talk & swear I can feel my brains melt down my throat. It tastes like burnt pancakes.

If I get clean Mom & Dad will you come back? Mom I'm cutting down on my swear words as you can see. Dad I told you I'm learning to fix Pieces. You don't have to answer right away just think about it ok?

I was going through your closets bc I don't have ~~shit all~~ much else to do & I found the old Scrapbook Mom made of me. I don't know why it was buried so deep but don't worry I wiped off the dust & grime. It has my baby pictures & a piece of my Blankie & report cards that say I'm Kind & a Peacemaker & all the stars I got for spelling words right & a picture of me as the Cowardly Lion & then So Many football stories. I felt Very Proud. There was also the article about how I saved the Fullerton kid which is another reminder I'm Kind & a Peacemaker. I'd text you photos of the Scrapbook except my contacts got wiped when the cops confiscated my phone & that is On Me. But if you want I can mail the Scrapbook so you can remember how Proud you were of me in the past.

You're probably thinking hey if Robbie can write a letter this long why didn't he write better papers for school but let me remind you it's Very Different when you're writing an essay for Mr. Toppen about The Man Who Corrupted

Hadleyburg vs. when you're writing a Personal Letter from your Heart. I know I should stop but I want to tell you although it made me Very Sad to be LEFT BEHIND I understand why you did it.

I haven't forgotten the Cocks & Balls painted on the driveway which were really realistic & the Human Feces wiped all over the garage & how they hung poor Frank Costanza the cat from the tree & the Fire Cocktail they fired into your bedroom by accident instead of mine bc I'm sure that was the Last Straw. I started this Very Long letter telling you everything's fine but that's a lie. Nothing's better. Everyone's still so Mad at me. When I go buy food people spit loogies on my legs.

I really messed things up didn't I? I suppose I'm like the Man That Corrupted Hadleyburg which starts off saying Hadleyburg was the nicest town ever before one guy messed it all up. I should have written my Hadleyburg essay about myself. I never did what Mr. Toppen said & that's On Me. He said stop writing "bc" bc life isn't a text message but I told him "bc" looked like a battle axe & that I needed battle axes to hack my way through life. He also said stop using "&" but to me "&" is a symbol meaning Keep Going & Don't Quit & Infinity & seeing it is like seeing I have a Future. Mr. Toppen & everyone else gave me bad grades & maybe that's why I tried so hard at football & maybe that's how all the Violence happened.

I really ~~fucked up~~ made mistakes Mom & Dad & I'm really sorry & don't blame you I was LEFT BEHIND & I understand if you don't want to come back until you're forced to by the Lawsuit but I hope you come back before then &

I'll have the Ginsu Cutlery Set & Seinfeld mug & the clocks just like you left them. One day I hope me & you who I will call Mom & Dad & not To Whom It May Concern can laugh about the Good Times & the Hard Times together in our spacious above ground pool.

Your Loving Son,
Robbie

Bugs

Robbie has a collection of clocks. I know it sounds like pussy stuff but dont hate on it till you hear me out. When his mom and pops took off to I dont know where and left behind Robbies sorry ass, all he had left was this house he grew up in and even though its crumbly now and everythings broke hes still got his pops legendary clock collection. Theres like fifty of those bitches. Ones a giant grandfather clock with a cabinet big enough to hide Midge. Theres cuckoo clocks with sheep dancing and birds singing and shorties carrying beers. Theres also clocks with Mickey Mouse and this dude Elvis and this black and white cat with moving eyes that dont tell anyone but freaks me out.

One thing Midget does in her spare time is take the clocks and mess them up speedwise and timewise so none a them are accurate, so when a bunch happen to go off at the same time its like a lucky sign, you know? Drives Robbie crazy though. The second we open Robbies door to leave, a bunch of clocks start dinging and donging and I pause to be appreciative. Omens like that increase your confidence and you need confidence before you walk down Yellow Street with a big fat wad a green. Yeah, its morning but lots a business goes down in the morning on Yellow Street. Junkies still wandering for a fix and hos that didnt make enough for their pimps. Us three are pretty hardcore for kids but it aint like none of us are packing chrome.

Best thing to do is lighten the mood with a humorous crack so right when the door shuts I turn to Dag and scream <Bitch, now hand over my money!> Dag laughs and laughs and laughs and she looks so fly in her fuzzy long skirt and her red jacket with all the zippers. Dang!

I style myself tight too. You dont need to worry about that. I thug a XXXL whitey so the hood rats know Im a hundred percent street. Havent laundried it for a few months but it dont smell too bad really. Then I super style it with a jean jacket I markered all over with the best lines from Fellowship of the Ring. The left arm says <DONT YOU LEAVE HIM SAMWISE GAMGEE> and the right arm says <THEY HAVE A CAVE TROLL> and the back says <I SWEAR TO YOU I WILL NOT LET THE WHITE CITY FALL, NOR OUR PEOPLE FAIL>. Lots of people make fun of my jacket, street people and school people and teacher people too. Theyre just jealous though cuz its the baddest ass jacket they ever witnessed and even if my markering isnt super neat I know I spelled everything correct cuz I checked the internet.

At least Dag and me dress proper for the cold. Midget hasnt dressed proper one day in her whole shrimpy little life. Today shes got on some dirty green sweatpants and a dirty green shirt. Her shoes are green too and I guarantee thats coincidence cuz Midge is too little to know anything about creating styles. Little sister isnt wearing a jacket, a hat, a scarf, nothing. Its Halloween, girl! Wind gets chilly! Its refreshing on my pinkeye but thats the only good thing about it.

Midge doesnt complain though. Midget never complains to nobody except bugs. You heard it right. Bugs, yo. Like insects. Its got so normal in my brain that its hard to remember how mightyducked up it is. Any time Midge gets excited or worked up, what she does is root around till she radars some bugs and then she whispers out her feelings. One thing Robbies cribs got a bunch of is bugs so I figure thats why she likes to go there so much.

I wish I was punking you but the whole things true. Midget has brain damage. Dont ask me how it happened. I dont really enjoy talking about it. I guess I mostly wonder what she tells the bugs. You think she talks about me? I guess thatd be all right. She talk about Moms too? And all a Moms big time troubles? I guess its nothing to stress on. Nothing at all. What do I care what some small little girl that isnt even my real sister says about Moms to a bunch a flies and centipedes?

We arent even off the stoop before Midge kneels down and investigates our jackolantern like shes from CSI Miami. Must be some beetles or worms up inside that big orange bitch. Moms bought it from some banger with a shopping cart full a pumpkins and even though it was fungused I was psyched cuz Moms hardly ever gets out of bed and when she does its only to cross the street to reup her cigs cuz the dude that works there wont let me buy any for her. Last time Moms acquired me something special like that was once upon a time and a galaxy far away.

I lugged that big orange bastard all the way down Yellow Street cuz Robbies got ten Ginsu knives hes super proud of and I knew theyd be perfect for doing pumpkins. Robbie warned me it was too early for carving and dang, yo, turns out fat boy was correct. Here its Halloween day and the jackolanterns mouth is sucked in like No Teeth Mike, this dude that shoots up across from school. Its all withered and rotten and a gross poop color. Every time I look at it I think about Moms cuz shes the one that bought it special for me and also cuz shes up in her room getting all withered and rotten too. Maybe Moms has bugs in her head like the jackolantern does? That would explain a lot.

Some things arent good to think on though so I yank up Midge by her green sweaties and give her a shove so we can get our show on the road. Right off I regret it cuz what if you can catch pinkeye off clothes? If Midget wakes up tomorrow with a crusty eye Im gonna suicide myself. So I let her run up ahead. Robbies lawn is soggy like the Dead Marshes Frodo almost drowned in but I got my snowboots on so I smash through it like one a them dozers that are everywhere.

Dag squeals cuz shes a girl. Now her tights have spots a mud. Sorry, Dag! Dags the whole reason Im even wearing snowboots in October. Dag taught me how snowboots are helpful when youre stealing a theft. If a uniform rolls up, hes not gonna think to check snowboots for stolen goods. Plus my boots have blue and silver stripes that are very fresh. Plus theyre comfortable. Plus I aint got any other shoes currently. People at school tease my snowboots but they can eat a dick.

Few blocks past the burnt down super fun to play in Taco Bell ruins we see Deformo pacing around under a underpass. Hes this super ugly ass malformed ass homeless dude that spooks me real dire cuz a his nasty ass deformed ass face. He used to hang out closer to Pinebluff Glenn Estates, begging for food and sleeping all over the dang place, but the dozers keep chasing him closer to Yellow Street.

I have nightmares about Deformo, for real. I dont know if his mom ate bowls a toxic waste when she was pregnant or what but hes a straight up horror movie monster. I aint ever seen him except from a distance and, yo, thats how my precautionary ass wants to keep it. Knowing Dag she might try to get all deep in discussion with that horror movie monster but thats not good for Midget. Deformo would give Midge bad dreams till she peed the bed. You got to be safety first when it comes to little bitches.

We hit the sidewalk and I put my fists in my jean jacket and glare down the block at Deformo so it looks like Im packing. Isnt a total lie either. I may not have a gat but I do have six ninja throwing stars from KBK Pawn on 33rd. Two a them are four point carbon steel. That sharkweek is no joke. But I also got a eight point shuriken, a six point kohga, a four point black ronin, and baddest of all a stainless steel ninja disc designed like a dragon with scythe blades. I had to theft forever to afford that one. But its a smart value cuz it came with a nylon pouch free a charge and good thing too cuz that sharkweek is sharp! If Deformo ever gets his gross ass too close hes gonna get ninjaed!

Out here you better be armed. Inside Robbies crib it doesnt matter cuz youre protected on all sides like Helms Deep. No orcs are gonna breach that stronghold! Once I cracked that joke to Dag and she hit me playful like shorties do and so I think about saying it again. Then I remember my pinkeye. I cant be letting Dag touch me today even though itd be nice. So I fall back and forget about pumpkin bugs and Moms and all a that troublesome junk and just watch Dags red zipper coat go bobbing down the street toward the dozers like she owns this whole bitch. Its too bad she dont want my wiener cuz sometimes shes pretty as hell.

My Wiener

My wieners all right. The lookout boys near 10th and Dawson saw it last summer after this fool Cabin Boy tricked me into dropping my drawers at the honeys across the way. We were all gonna do it, least thats what Cabin Boy said, but when we got to the count a three no robocops dropped their drawers except me. Then Cabin Boy hopped around and laughed and pointed. I tried to play it like a pimp but he kept saying how my wiener was the size of a peanut. Dang! You cant throw shade on Jody like that! If Cabin Boy didnt have a hundred pounds on me plus that strap in his belt I woulda gone ape on that bitch! Instead I ended up all worried. What if one day Dag decides to hit it with me like Robbie hit it with Little Lamb and Dag finds out I got a peanut dick? So I went down to Pop Nates and got me a bag of shell peanuts and measured it out by the dumpster. And my junk was three times as big, yo! Still small next to Cabin Boy probably, but look, man, Im young. I havent had my growth spurt yet. You best watch your ass cuz one a these days my wiener will be living large and robocops will stop picking on me and girlies will be nice to me and finally everything will be all right.

Gwendolyn

Halfway to Walgreen Deformos way out a sight and we run across Gwendolyn. Shes the illest dog alive. She has this tangle ass, muddy ass fur that hangs from her belly and a crooked tail and usually shes limping with a hurt paw. Bitchs eyes are more pink and gooey than mine. This dog loves Dag cuz Dag feeds it. Every time we find the yucky mutt Dag pulls out some baggie full a Better Cheddars or Triscuits. Dags the one that gave it its dumb name too. Gwendolyn? For real? Id a called it Dracula cuz that bitchs been around forever and is still kicking.

The tragic fact is Gwendolyn never lets Dag close enough to pet it. Us three are in this junked out lot that used to be a grocery and Gwendolyns hiding between a broke Big Wheel and a busted drum from like a drum kit. Dag whips out a bag a Nacho Cheese Pretzel Combos. Right away I start bugging. Combos? You serious? I woulda ate the crap outta those Combos! Combos are ideal for breakfast cuz it has pretzel, which is mostly the same as toast, and also cheese. Cheese is straight up health food.

But Dags not thinking about me. She steps real quiet and pours the bag out by the manhole. Then she backs up till Gwendolyn drags her ass out and gives it a sniff. Of course the dog decides to eat my Combos but she keeps her red eyes on Dag the whole while like shorty might shank her. The whole things dumb. Dags about to cry with emotion and Midgets holding on to my leg super tight cuz she takes after whatever Dag do. Its like all a us are watching the miracle of life or some sharkweek when all any a us are doing is watching a scabby ass mongrel snarf up my dang breakfast.

Gwendolyns busy licking the cement so Dag takes a big breath and edges close like always. Look, Ill be straight with you. Mostly I want that dog to chill. Dags been trying to pet that bitch two years now and if she really wants to put her hands on some filthy ass fur thats her personal business. Same time, though, the look on Dags face, it bothers me, yo. It does. She looks like shes in love with the stupid animal. It probably has a billion fleas and diseases. Dags got a few problems like sister Lotte being in a nuthouse but shes from Pinebluff Glenn Estates and should know better. Its like with Deformo. Even if Dag dont care about herself one bit, Midget needs protecting. Midgets a small ass child that already gets sick all the time and medicine is mad expensive, just ask Moms.

The whole situation gets me feeling a itch so I end up busting out my eight point shuriken. I wipe away my infected eye crust so I can see good and get my stance proper so I can throw real accurate and Dag gasps like Ive gone insane. Right before I throw she does like a girl and goes <No! Jody, no! Jody, dont!> Whys she got to embarrass me like that? I throw my shuriken anyway and it zings off the curb next to Gwendolyn. Scares that animal serious. Bitch runs.

For real, all I meant to do was scare it. But Dags pissed. She starts railing about how you dont throw lethal ninja objects at innocent animals and what was I thinking and am I some kinda sicko. Its too early in the dang day to get yelled at by someone thats not Robbie! So I stand tough and ask if she wants Midget to acquire rabies and have to go get needles in her stomach to get unrabied cuz thats how they do it. Dag looks like shes gonna punch me in the mouth.

She goes <Thats really why you threw it? Look at me and tell me thats really why you threw it.>

When a ho starts crowding Jody, thats when a ho needs to get owned! Now dont get me wrong. Girlfriend is right. Girlfriend knows shes right. But that doesnt matter when youre talking about pride.

So shes hollering in my grill and the itch in my head is getting itchier and the situations about to go to the next level and thats when Midget starts tugging my finger. Dang! Dang! I pull it back real quick. But Midge is just trying to give me back my eight point shuriken she rescued off the pavement. Thats some real sweet generous behavior.

I wipe my infection finger on my jean jacket and go <Thank you, little bitch> cuz back in the day Moms said you need to positive reinforce a child thats messed up like Midge. Even though Im mad at Dag I look at her and Dags looking at Midge the same way she looked at Gwendolyn. Thats all it takes for my feelings to switch up and that hot itch inside me to quit itching. The three a us are fam. You feel me? You ever had fam? Well then you know just how it goes.

Dearest Lotte,

How are you? I would like to respond to your many queries. Firstly, Morrissey, Johnny, Andy, and Mike the fish are fine! I detect you are distraught about them but please don't be. They are darting around their spic-and-span fish bowl, happily gobbling the fish food I sprinkle them, and seem happy. Wait, can fish be happy, ha ha ha? In one of your letters, you said the Clinic was a fish bowl for humans. Excellent metaphor, Lotte! If that's still true, consider adopting the upbeat attitudes of Morrissey, Johnny, Andy, and Mike, ha ha ha.

Let me progress through your other questions speedily. Here we go! Yes, I did get Mr. Cartwright for Home Room, and I see what you mean, but he's been nice to me so far. No, sigh, I'm not even wearing a training bra. It's just a padded sports bra, which doesn't even have letters and numbers. Just Large, Medium, and Small, and Microscopic special made for me, ha ha ha. No, I have not seen "Deadgirl," "Antichrist," or "Martyrs," but I know where you keep your Blu-Rays and I'll check them out! Yes, Papa still keeps the stock market channel on all day, barfffff. Yes, Mama's still considering a maid, but I think that's unlikely since the Clinic is costing so much money.

Lotte, you wrote so many questions! It makes me laugh because when you lived here you never asked questions at all. Therefore I hate to say this, but can I answer the rest later? If I answer them all now, I'll run out of purple ink, and you know how I love my purple ink.

You may not realize it, but I just got all your letters dumped on me at once. Is this sisterly correspondence or a novel?! That's six months of letters—and I read them all. Mama collected them in a shoebox (for one of her mile-long high heels of course). Don't be mad, OK? Mama explained they didn't want your letters distracting me from schoolwork and extra-curriculars. Now, I admit I <u>did</u> wonder why you weren't writing and I <u>was</u> getting a little upset. But everything is splendiferous now! Well, you're still in the Clinic, but besides that, ha ha ha.

I should probably be what Papa calls a "straight shooter" and tell you that Mama and Papa are reading this letter. (Hi Mama and Papa.) That's OK with me, and I hope it's OK with you. I for one don't have any deep dark secrets to share. Unless you count the thrilling news about my sports bra, ha ha ha.

Mama said I can write you for your birthday (June 6) and Christmas. These limits are to help me focus on schoolwork and extra-curriculars. It sounds sad, I know, but I think it's working. Every time I get down in the dumps about you being all alone in the Clinic, boop! It's time to go to an extra-curricular! I have so many new ones. Let's see, there's Coding Club, Junior Robotics, High Voltage Dance Troupe, Future Problem Solvers, Lincoln-Douglas Debate Squad…and that's just some of them! Anyway, I hope you'll be home before

Christmas so I won't have to write you a letter ever again, j/k, ha ha ha.

(How are you enjoying the letter, Mama and Papa? Are you impressed I haven't talked Lotte into doing something crazy like take the doctors and nurses hostage and make them perform Swan Lake in their underwear? Lotte, remember when Papa took us to see Swan Lake? Ugh, I can't stand how pretty the dancers were. That's not the kind of dancing we do in the High Voltage Dance Troupe, I can tell you that!)

Hmm, what else is going on? Things are status quo at good old Pinebluff Glenn Estates. You remember when we moved into "The Glenn" and it was about twenty houses? There must be two hundred now. I must apologetically report that the bulldozer noise, which you loved to block out with your headphones, is still an issue. At least it's farther away now. The bulldozers look like little yellow bugs eating up the neighborhood to the south. Remember it? The roads all have color-based names, like Red Street and Blue Street, which I thought was pretty until Mama said it was because no one cared enough to think of real street names.

To be a straight shooter, I <u>know</u> you remember it. That's where you got into some of your trouble. We don't have to talk about that, Lotte. I bet you talk about it with your therapists until you're blue in the face. At night when I'm snuggled in with Clara Bear McGrumpy, I dream of walking over to that neighborhood to find out exactly what you did, except I don't walk there, I zoom like an insect. (Have no fear, Mama and Papa, I won't actually do it.)

Please don't interpret that as me asking to know the nature of your troubles. If you told me, Mama and Papa would only intercept it anyway. I only know one detail about your troubles, but it's a detail I know very, very, very well. When I think back on finding you, I don't remember dialing 911 or trying to get you to throw up. All I remember feeling is like I was the one about to die. I could barely move my limbs. I think it was because I was so sad. For so long I thought you were angry at us for moving to The Glenn. But it turns out you weren't angry at all! You were lonely and scared!

Even though it's a prudent choice not to let me visit the Clinic (hi Mama and Papa), I do wish I had Spider-Man abilities and could scale the walls and crawl into your bed like olden days, and snuggle you like Clara Bear McGrumpy. Would you even like that? Are you still not into touching people? Are you different now? Look, now I'm the one asking all the questions, ha ha ha.

I think I'm becoming different too.

I'm sorry this letter isn't cheerier. I'm sorry it's written on spiral notebook paper, which probably reminds you of Our Lady of Heavenly Blessing. Next time I'll buy some decorative stationery. You said the Clinic is a beigepocalypse, and I know that was a joke, but it's also the saddest detail I've heard so far. I never agreed with Mama (sorry, Mama) that your room here is too black. There's a ton of red too if you look! Red lipstick, red nail polish, red curtains, red headphones, red skull decals, red posters, red bras, a red lightbulb in your lamp, and let's not forget one of your fish is red, though I don't know if it's Morrissey, Johnny, Andy, or Mike, ha ha ha.

Well, I better wrap it up, it's time for piano lessons. Thrilling, huh? I know you can be as stubborn as a mule, but listen to your doctors, try to make friends, and choke down as much beige food as possible, ha ha ha. Mama and Papa miss you even if they don't say it much. What they do say all the time is how much the Clinic costs, and that's why I'm at PS 220 now instead of Our Lady of Heavenly Blessing. Surprise! Don't worry about me, I've already made pals with a kid named Jody. I think you'd like him. He sees things differently than most people, just like you.

Your little sister who misses you,
Dagmar

P.S. Oh, I almost forgot! Mama told me to say that suicide is never the answer, you can always talk to a trusted adult, there are free hotlines to call with trained counselors, you're just depressed, some people have it much worse than you, and if you succeeded think of what it would do to your family.

Midget

Dag and me must be feeling charitable to Midget cuz the rest a the walk we include her in our conversation, real interesting stuff like do peoples heads pop off when they get hanged and whats up with yeast infections and how its possible from like a science perspective for Aragorn to surf down the bones of the Dead Men of Dunharrow. We go like <Isnt that right, Midget?> and <Midget, you hear that?> and <I bet Midget knows what Im saying!> Course Midge doesnt reply. Shes busy trying to trap a fly in her hand so she can tell it her secrets. But I think she enjoys hearing her name in chitchat. When we cross the street little sister holds real tight to my jean jacket.

Midget doesnt do squat unless her bug friends say its all right. Makes life challenging around the homefront, Ill tell you what. If I want her to take out a trash bag I got to wait for her to catch a fly first and have a whole long discussion about it. By then the trash is dripping all over! One time Midge cupped her hand by her ear to hear fly secrets and that fly zoomed right up inside. Moms about crapped her drawers. She started thumping Midges skull to knock the fly out and when that didnt work she poked a chopstick in there. Finally she dragged Midge to a doc in the box and Moms was crying all hysterical and I was like <Moms, why you tripping?> and Moms says she saw a picture in a book that showed maggots crawling out a ear cuz a fly laid eggs inside it and if Midget starts hatching maggots in her ear the city robocops are gonna take her away and there go our monthly checks.

The doc though just flushes the fly out with oil. Yo, the craziest part? Midge was happy as hell with that bug in her brain. She was grinning like it was Christmas, nodding real interested like the fly was giving her important knowledge. But when it flushed out all oily and dead Midge worked herself up like I never saw. Moms was afraid to even touch her emotional ass. And that was back when Moms still acted mostly normal and didnt spend all day talking to the TV.

A few months after we got Midget I was bored as hell and I told myself, Jody, its time to solve The Mystery of Midget. So I went all 007 and strapped on the goggles I found in Robbies yard and put on my high class Isotoner gloves I discovered in the weeds and took off my snowboots for super stealth and then I creeped across our crib. The carpets always nasty with tater chips but 007 never complains. I snaked my ass over to Midgets room and listened to her whisper to her bugs for like half a day and the only word I comprehended was <DAndre>. Midgets giggling <DAndre> this and <DAndre> that. So much boring ass garbage I fell asleep right there in my goggles till Midget woke my ass up cuz she was hungry. Little sister likes her butter bread with sugar.

So check this. About a year back Dag thefted some bags from Taco Bell and we were on the monkey bars at 15th and Clinton killing those bags dead and she starts in with her gordita grease mouth about how Moms told her a story about Midge. Even though Dags from Pinebluff Glenn Estates she comes to the hood sometimes and her and Moms are friendly and discuss things private. It never bothered me cuz I figured it was about maxi pads or babies or how come her jugs are so small. Turns out it was confidential stuff Moms didnt even tell her dang son! I started chucking taco supremes and cheesy fiesta potatoes far as I could cuz that raged me up.

What Dag learned is Moms isnt the first foster mom to get Midget. One lady that took Midget also took this child DAndre and when I heard that I thought <Uh oh!> but I kept it to myself cuz remember I was feeling rageful. Dag said this lady also had real biologic children that were mean as hell and one day they pushed DAndre off the roof and DAndre busted his arm. Even though Midget was crying for help the real children didnt want to get in trouble so they went to where this orange vest robocop was paving the sidewalk and the little fools jacked them some wet cement and cemented up DAndres arm.

I heard a lot of wack junk before but dang. Foster lady must a been in worse shape than Moms if she didnt notice her new foster boy had a cement cast out of nowhere. Either that or she didnt care. Few days in, DAndres arm went ripe. Children couldnt even sleep cuz a the stink. Plus DAndre was screaming like a bitch how they had to get that cement off him so finally the kids found a hammer and cracked off a chunk and a big chunk a DAndres rotted ass arm came off with it. Now all of them were screaming.

But heres the most important detail. There were like a hundred flies under there. They cracked off that cement and flies exploded all over. Maggots were present too. Maggots are baby flies in case you arent an expert on insects. Look, Im no 007, not for real, but Im just saying there could be a connection between Midges current ways and all this traumatic garbage from her screwed up history.

Walgreen

This one raw old black dude is the Walgreener we hate most and of course hes working the register. Dag and me call him Dick Trickle cuz one time Dag saw that name in the Walgreen newspaper rack. Dick Trickles bony like hes whittled from a stick and he has a bunch a old ass ties and thick ass glasses and a balding ass old man fro. Hes mean as a wasp. The cashier we were hoping for is this white bitch with bionic arm canes thats blind as hell. Usually I ask a complicated question about the products they stack up front like the Slanket or the Lint Lizard or the Ahh Bra and meantime Dag sneaks around and loads up on cigs. But you cant steal nothing off Dick Trickle. Robocop boxes you out like hes Dwight Howard.

Dick Trickle hates it when three youths come in simultaneous and hes got his beady eyes all over our asses. I get Dag to hand me Robbies chip and I wave that paper like a pimp. See this green? Im gonna buy all your candies, homes! Dick Trickle just shakes his old ass head like we stole the bills straight from his register. Whatever, man. Go back to policing your stupid smokes.

First thing Dag always does is browse the beautiful papers for people to write letters. They have designs like flowers and blue skies and a dog sitting his dog ass on a beautiful beach. Dags sister Lotte doesnt have real internet in the nuthouse, so Dag writes letters old school and she likes them to look pretty so Lotte has pretty things to enjoy. Dag says in the psych ward the only TV and books they have are inspirational. I asked how about magazines and she said the only magazine they have is Oprah magazine. Dag says she writes to Lotte about me and Midget and all our adventures. It makes me so proud I can hardly explain it.

But this isnt the time to be purchasing beautiful papers. No doubt Robbies filling Yellow Street with cuss words cuz a how late we are with his candies. But hold up. Oh, hell yes! Theres a whole aisle a Halloween masks, and Im sorry Robbie but masks this fine have got to be worn! Even though tonights Halloween Walgreens still got a nice big selection, probably cuz nobody comes to this crap ass Walgreen except when they need a jimmy hat or rash cream or something else real immediate.

Dag puts on a rubber monster face almost as bad as Deformo. Dang, Dag! Take that scary junk off! Midgets hiding her frightened ass so I put on a discount Barack Obama head and go after little sister cuz this a good opportunity for education. Man, I love Barack Obama. Barack Obama is a straight up American hero. Dont tell anybody cuz theyd tease me but I like to think about Barack Obama being my dad. Like maybe he knew Moms before he got famous. Why the hell not? Some cool ass black dude with sharp ass robocop suits that talked super smooth and believed in my future and filled me with hope and change.

I find Midge over by the cherry cough drops and lecture her how Barack Obama used to be the chief mightyducker of the whole US of A not to mention the stone cold robocop that killed the dude that did the twin towers. Little sister gets confused cuz usually Im lecturing her about the Two Towers from Lord of the Rings and now she probably thinks Barack Obama killed Sauron. Politics are mad complex.

Nobody enjoys stank ass rubber tasting masks like Dag. Now shes a wolfman and then a devil and then an alien. Stuff is pricey, though. We add up our money and we dont have enough to even cover one mask, not if we get Robbie his candy. Dag chucks her mask on the floor with all the other masks she chucked. Midget starts cleaning them up but I yank her ass back. Hell, no. Dick Trickle can pick it up himself. Hes the one charging too much, aint he? For now though I keep wearing Barack Obama cuz it makes me feel good. Any terrorist I roll across is gonna get his ass wasted.

Even though shes flinging masks Dag isnt upset for real and I know why. She has herself a secret costume shes been keeping secret. I been begging for clues for weeks but girlfriends skillful at keeping secrets. I bet shes constructing herself a princess thing or a fairy deal and is gonna show up tonight looking so fly Ill be like dang! There isnt hardly nothing Dag cant do. Ever since Lotte got her ass locked away Dags folks make her take lessons in every subject you can think of. She can tap dance like a mightyducker. Play the sharkweek out a some piano too. Shortys talented as hell!

Thats when I have the idea to fix me a costume too. I know Dags been slaving on hers a whole month and I only have a few hours but the idea blows up my brain. Grishnákh! Bitch is my favorite ass orc! I know some internet robocops are preferential to Gorbag cuz a his armor, which I admit is sweet, but those are the same robocops that forget how Gorbag pussied out after Frodo got his Hobbit ass cocooned by Shelob and how that led to Gorbag getting impaled by Samwise Gamgee. Think about it, yo. Remember when Grishnákh disobeyed Uglúk and tried to eat Pippin and Merry and got himself speared? Dude didnt flinch at all. Grishnákhs just a short little killer like me but it took Treebeard to pop his ass, didnt it?

So while Dags busy fishing Midget out of a bin a plastic snakes I scrounge me up some Grishnákh teeth and shove them down my snowboot. Grishnákh has a purple face so I scrounge me some face paint too. The purple is a little off. It isnt rotted skin purple. Its brighter. Its got a picture of a girl done up like a Care Bear. But I bet itll do all right. I rip it outta the pack and snowboot it. The final thing I need is a yellow wig but that isnt gonna happen. Even old ass Dick Trickle will notice if theres yellow hair poofing out my boot.

Dags gonna poop her pants when she sees! Last winter I got shorty to watch the whole award winning saga. Took six weeks to get through cuz Dag kept forgetting to bring her laptop to Robbies and when she did she kept falling asleep. She said she wasnt bored, just confused. What I did was turn on the subtitles for education purposes. That didnt work either! I was elbowing her pretty much constant cuz important plot stuff goes down all the dang time in Lord of the Rings. Things got better once I said it was all right if she painted her nails or texted her mom, but honestly it made me wonder if she was even enjoying Peter Jacksons cinematic masterpiece. But she told me she did and that made me feel tight. No doubt she remembers Grishnákh. No doubt!

We go to the candy aisle and the candy aisle is banging. Its got all your Halloween basics like Reeses Peanut Butter Pumpkins, Ghost Dots, Cadbury Screme Eggs, Pumpkin Peeps. Its got Brachs Party Mix which is great value for your dollar. Also Hershey Kiss Pumpkin Spice thats tasty as hell even though it sounds super gross. Best thing about Walgreen though is they stock crazy off brand junk too. Max o Malt and Choco Crisp plus Gummy Body Parts and Spooky Lip Pops and this interesting product called Blood Bag thats candified gel you squeeze out a tube. Im feeling supermilked just imagining the taste sensations.

Me and my crew get a basket and load up. Midget wants Twirl Pops with spider and ghost designs. You dont got to ask twice, Midge! Dag wants her some ancient chalky old Twilight Sweethearts that are like normal Sweethearts except they have Twilight words like <BE MY BLLA> and <I♥EC>. I dont have a clue what that means but who cares? In the basket it goes!

Now dont worry. We dont forget Robbies Fun Size Snickers. Dag, though, shes smarter than all our asses, especially fat boy, and she starts thinking logical. If Robbie really wants to put crack rock inside candy bars, he didnt choose very wise, did he? What do they say about Snickers on TV? They say Snickers are packed with peanuts! And if its packed with peanuts, theres not gonna be much room for crack rock, you know?

Dag ponders for a bit and says what we need is Three Musketeer cuz Three Musketeer is like ninety percent nougat. Dags so intelligent I decide to ask her why she figures Robbie really wants to hand out drugged up candies in the first place and Dag just repeats how Robbie hates people cuz how they did him wrong in the past. Seems kind a overboard if you ask me but like I said shortys smarter than me by a mile so I go along. So we swap in Fun Size Three Musketeers and I feel so good about it I can take off Barack Obama without feeling too sad. I even wipe the inside of the mask on my pants cuz I dont want the next inspirational American that wears it to be catching pinkeye.

Dick Trickle

The register lines dragging balls. We have to wait behind all your regular fools. Cameltoe skanks and sports jersey bros. When we get next in line I tiptoe to peep the snap of Robbie they have taped up. But Midget starts pestering me with her hungry whine so I take out the Dubble Bubble. This time a year Dubble Bubble has sick styles like Slime Balls and Horror Eyes and little sister cant resist, so I rip open the bag and fetch her one. Dick Trickle frowns so hard I think his dentures are gonna pop out.

Wheezy ass darth breather mightyducker scans our candies. What gets me provoked is how he looks at Dag and Midge. Like hes sympathetic to them on account a my sorry ass. Cuz Midgets a small ass little child? Cuz Dags got nice clothes and done up hair? Dick Trickle doesnt know the first dang thing about me! He doesnt know that back when Moms used to do stuff normal I looked more proper. He doesnt know that my pops was probably a Barack Obama robocop thats ten times the bad ass Dick Trickle is. And that means I am too. I got those Barack Obama genes inside me. Around Yellow Street, that gives me all the cred I need.

When I whip out Robbies chip, Dick Trickle inspects it close with his thick ass glasses. Whats this dudes malfunction? I do my thug face but he just fronts with his scratched ass nametag and his veiny ass hands trembling cuz hes super old. He shakes his head like hes disappointed and bags our candies and sends our change down the change slide. Midget loves the change slide and Dag boosts her so she can catch it. That right there is childlike joy, yo. That sharkweek is priceless. And I cant even enjoy it, Im so heated. When I take the bag I say <Thanks, my robocop> except I dont say <robocop>, I say what Robbie calls the Forbidden Word cuz I figure I got a right to use it, at least half a right if Im imagining my pops right.

Believe, yo. I didnt think it would rile him up that much! Dick Trickle goes off like a warhead. Geezer reaches across the scanner and claws hold a my jean jacket. Candy bag falls right outta my hand. It takes a sec before I even know what the hell. Next thing I know Im flopping around like a fish but the old dude has fists a steel. He pulls me half on the counter and leans down his gnarly ass face and goes <What did you say to me?> I get my expletives going cuz its starting to hurt, and Dick Trickle gets squinty like he cant hear good and he goes <What are you even saying? What are you even saying?>

Where does he get off handling a juvenile like that? Im not crying. Im not. Dudes dog breath in my face is whats got me moisturized. All I know is Im yelling for Dag to hail down a uniform which is a crazy play considering all the Grishnákh gear Ive got snowbooted. My mind isnt right. Its all wrong. Its itching like crazy. I got my hand in my jacket where I keep my ninja stars and I can feel my six point kohga all sharp on my fingers. What am I gonna do with it? What am I gonna do? I dont know, I cant tell, I cant even tell.

Dags the one that saves the day. She pulls my hand right outta the pocket. Right then Dick Trickle lets me go. My face is all hot and I know I must look like a pink faced bitch so I try to pop back and call him out. But all the tough ass sharkweek I want to say comes out all stuttery and stupid. Dudes not even paying attention. Hes staring all guilty over by the Slankets where theres this pissed looking white dude with a weak ass goatee and a beer belly and a nametag that says <MANAGER>.

I get a laugh outta that! Manager isnt even Robbies age! And he looks like hes about to can Old Man Trickle. Probably has concerns I might sue their Walgreen asses. Dang straight! Moms has watched so many Judge Judys and Judge Mathises by now shes probably a expert at litigating and cross examining and all that. I think we should stick around and watch goatee manager man give Dick Trickle the business but Dags yanking my wrist and Midgets spitting out her Dubble Bubble and its true Im itching fierce. What I could use right now to chill me out is a big tall glass a supermilk.

Scrapbook

Can I be honest with you? After that crap with Gwendolyn and that Walgreen crap I feel better once we get past all the growling dozers and see Robbies great big dump castle. Feels like Im where no ones gonna tell me what I am and what Im not. First thing I always see when coming up the way is this big huge satellite dish from Robbies parents yesteryears. Its always full up with rain and Midget splashes around in there when its warm and her ass always comes out black and oily. I have to hose her down and she dances around in the hose water real funny. We make some special memories no doubt.

Maybe its nasty but this crib feels more like home than home feels like home. I constructed a pleasant ass walking path out a tire flaps that have pictures a sexy women and Foghorn Leghorn and it goes from the satellite dish to a wall we built out a car batteries tall as hell. From time to time, Robbie comes out in his drawers to smoke and professors about those batteries. He says that right theres the negative terminal and thats the vent cap and thats the sediment chamber and Im like, bitch, nobody cares! This is our wall now and its kicking!

Robbie keeps his rims around back. I know people are serious about rims, but even a architecture up and comer like me cant build anything good from them. Me and Dag and Midget prefer the mad junk nobody can comprehend how Robbies pops even knew how to fix. You ever seen a typewriter? Man, its nuts. Theres a saxophone back there too. Still gold but you cant make it play. Robbie says its missing a reed so Midge and me took it apart. The typewriter too. We spread all the whole alphabet across this weird table that has all these cranks and dials. You just know Robbie had to act smart about that too. He says its a lithographic press. Fat boy, what? Shut the hell up before you embarrass yourself.

Truth is though Robbies crib educates better than school. Hes got a depth gauge from some kind a deep sea deal. Also a bridle that you put on a dang horse. Also a sundial so old its like from Jesus times. One of the baddest objects I found personally is a electrical meter. You have to unscrew about fifty screws and that takes dedication but then you get to see a million little gears and coils and technologies hid inside.

Picking through all that junk is relaxing. It makes me recollect when I used to see Miss Poole the school psychiatrist every Tuesday before she gave up. Miss Poole was a real nice latina lady with interesting titties that started counseling my troubled ass after I tried to help pull out a kids loose tooth with the arts and crafts scissors. Miss Pooles main job was inventing stuff to calm down my itch. Breathing yoga style and counting ass backward and imagining a boat in a lake, all kinds a funny junk. Well, Miss Poole, this electrical meter does the trick. Messing with all the complicated parts makes me want to go get a job in science so I can hypothesize concepts and theories and experiments.

When you play with this junk you imagine it being all bright and new like it used to be. Robbie cant fix nothing. Hes a grown ass adult and far as I know he dont have a single dang talent. He told me once hes not worried cuz hes got an aunt who won an internet contest for a house on a caribbean island but the aunts too sick to use it and said Robbie can have it since hes blood. Only Robbie cant claim it just yet because of tax reasons and government rules and this problem he calls red tape. Robbie says he has email proof and everything. I dont know. I havent seen it.

Truth is, I got worries. Punk ass bitch hasnt had income since Little Lamb left. Been a year at least. Even though I dig his crib the situation inside is bleak. Some weeks theres no power. Some weeks theres no water. When the toilets are dry me and Midget have to go squat in the backyard garbage. Dominos and Hardees and Dunkin Donuts trash tall as your ass. Of course theres flies too but I guess for Midge thats a bonus.

What Im sick a most is the mice. Its like Robbies parents left Robbie the house and he couldnt even keep hold of it. The mice stole it right from him. They rule the whole thing now even if you cant hardly see them under the trash. I step on one of their wiggly little asses about once a week. You ever hear a mouse scream? Sharkweek like that will give you nightmares. Believe.

One time I reached in one a the holes in the wall cuz I guess Im a stupid bitch. Robbies walls have holes all over from when he gets mad and karates everything. Anyway I reached in and it felt like hot mac and cheese but it ended up being a nest a mice, tiny pink babies with skin like bruises and that dont have eyes yet. It made me almost throw up so I found some McDonald salt packs and poured it all over those yucky little bitches cuz I know thats how you melt a snail. Next time I checked all there was was bones. But Robbie said it wasnt the salt that did it, it was cuz the bigger mice eat the littler mice. Was that supposed to make me feel better?

Robbies on his own dealing with the mice and all a his other problems cuz like I said, Robbies folks, wherever they are, dont talk to him. Lately Robbies been pawning his dads clocks, so you know his financials are rough. The clocks are the best dang things in the entire whole house. Ask anybody that lives on Yellow Street and theyll tell you how this situations gonna play out. One day the city will haul Robbies furniture and what clocks hes got left to the curb and board up the joint. What happens to Robbie then? Where are me and Midge and Dag supposed to go after that? Maybe its a positive thing the dozers are bashing closer every day.

A while back, I dropped my push pop in Robbies parents old room and when I reached under the trash I found this giant size scrapbook with materials from Robbies fabulous youth.

Tons a newspaper clips and snaps of him in a bad ass helmet and awards that said <MVP>. Dang! I hid that scrapbook way under Robbies folks bed cuz it just made me sad. Nobody oughta drag that out to the curb where people might see it. Nobody needs to see that thing ever again.

Apples

Robbie promised us, he did, I remember it perfect, he said take your asses to Walgreen and fetch me my candies and Ill fix you supermilks. But that promise does not occur. Instead he treats our bag a candy like its a bag a dog crap. Fat boy tosses it on the counter beside his beer empties and soft packs. Then he snaps his fingers for his change. Thats straight up rude cuz Midgets real excited about having change and its not worth upsetting a tiny little child for sixty two stupid cents. Midge doesnt ever cry but I can tell when shes sad. After all I live with the bitch.

I oughta be steaming mad but Robbies changed into my favorite shirt and that gives me optimism. Its a tank top and when he wears it you get to see his sorry ass discount tats and how theyre malforming cuz a the growing flab. You also get to see how his arms and chest are all smooth. Thats cuz fat boy practices Total Body Hair Removal. Robbie says its some kind a buddha thing to remove barriers between your body and mind. Robbie also says bitches like it. Ha! Hairless ass fat boy never sexed a bitch except Little Lamb and she said it was crap. If you ask me, Total Body Hair Removal has the opposite effect. It causes pimples and rashes. Robbie pretty much never stops itching his balls.

What makes the shirt my favorite shirt is it promotes a music group nobodys ever heard of. The band has itself a fly name, though. Barenaked Ladies! But before you start downloading their songs, let me explain that Barenaked Ladies are the saddest ass group of ugly ass pussies I ever saw. Two a these dicks have big ass glasses! One a them has dreads so bad its like a nightmare! And one a them is fat like Robbie! I bet even the whitest white dude in the world would look at these dudes and laugh his ass off. But if you criticize, Robbies face reds up and he defends them real hard, slobbering about how theyre underrated artistically and a bunch a other hilarious stuff. See why the shirt puts me in a positive mood?

Midget stands on her head by the wall cuz shes practicing for school. Little sister has real skills when it comes to standing on her head. Plus for a bonus, lots a times theres bugs on the floor. Dag and me are starving though, its ten and we havent had a single nutrient. We aint ate half as much as Gwendolyn the ugly dog. You know Im eyeing those candies we just bought but Robbie will hulk out if we help ourself. So I check the fridge and all its got is ketchup and last time I squirted ketchup in my mouth Dag gagged like she might puke.

Robbie shoves over all the stuff on the table. Mostly bowls with ants drowned in milk. Next he plops down a fancy basket a apples. Apples? Fat boy, youre crazy. First off, where did you acquire a fancy ass basket? Second, why did you buy like twelve dang apples? Robbie hates fruit. We all hate fruit. Next he plops down this busted up kleenex box that makes a rattle sound. Its been a time since I saw that box but

I remember it for sure. Its where Robbie keeps his razor blades for cutting blow. Man, its been infinity since Robbie had any blow. Thats one of the best supermilk ingredients in history. Gets your ass lifted quick.

When fat boy gets proud he sweats. Barenaked Ladies are clinging to his boobs. He says while the three a us were out lollygagging he hatched a brainstorm. What we should do, he says, is slide these razor blades into these fresh apples cuz think a how difficult itd be to detect. I guess me and Dag are just staring at him cuz he frustrates his face up and says how apples will work best cuz unwrapped candies look suspicious. He waits for our asses to agree but just being honest I dont know. Been a long ass time since Robbie was a child, you know? When I find candy on the sidewalk thats even got bites missing I still eat it. Dont tell Dag, yo.

Robbie puts a apple in one hand, a blade in the other, and then he takes a minute to reflect on the angles and whatnot. Im about to suggest he tap the blade in with like a hammer but thats when Dag loses her mind. Her fuss over Gwendolyn dont even compare. Shes all bawling and snotting and thrashing. Robbie has a sweet set of NFL magnets I keep ranked accurate on the fridge and just like that Dags arm wipes out the whole AFC North. Steelers and Browns and Bengals flying every which way. She kicks a cabinet and you can hear the mice family inside run off scared. She punches the wall too, right on the light switch so the lights flicker like all a us are in a horror movie and this is when one a us gets macheted.

Robbies speechless. Yo, me too. Me too, yo. Midget gets herself rightside up and I give her a smile so she isnt scared. Dag gets like this sometime. The girl has deep feelings inside. It makes me wish she had some female bitches for friends cuz female bitches understand how to handle freakouts. Me and Robbie arent skilled on the subject. We stand there like chumps while the light just goes on and off and on and off.

You cant punch a light switch long before your knuckles get torn up. I get stomach pains cuz a how the light switch starts getting all these little red smears. I guess Midget experiences it too cuz she starts squeaking. That doesnt sit right with me cuz Im her brother now and even if Im just a kid and mad short and have pinkeye I still have to man up and stand tall.

So I go up to Dag and say real sensitive <Dag, hold up, we got you, my bitch> and that must be the magic words cuz she looks at me passionate with her pretty wet eyelashes before she takes a glare at all them apples. For a second I think I got it worked out in my mind. Dags upset cuz she doesnt like Robbies Halloween plan after all, she thinks its mean to children that dont deserve dangerous drugs and razor blades. And I think thats a real interesting perspective.

Turns out though thats not what shes sobbing about at all. She starts telling off Robbie about how hes trying to ruin her Halloween cuz once word gets out some cheap ass mightyducker on Yellow Street is handing out fruits, wont any children bother coming to the house at all cuz handing out fruits on Halloween, thats some shameful ass sharkweek.

Dags got some lip on her, right? Anyhow it explains her whole big fit. Girlfriends been slaving on her secret costume for weeks and there wont be any point to wearing it if no one comes around to see it.

Fat boys dumbfounded. He looks like we stole his binkie. Dags still hollering and Midges still squeaking and Robbie starts pressing his hands over his ears. And its weird, yo. I get this video in my brain how all a Midgets private bug buddies hid themself inside Robbies skull and now theyre instructing his fat ass to do various sorts a odd junk, including this whole plan about fixing up dangerous candies, and now fat boys trying to keep those evil bugs from spilling out his ears.

Robbie smacks himself on the head and says he bought these mightyducking apples at the overpriced price the mightyducking market man was selling and he will be danged if theyre gonna go to waste. He smacks himself a few more times till his faces so red it looks like hes embarrassed instead a pissed and thats when I understand the whole ballgame. The chubby ass lying ass assbutt never called his new dealer! Thats why he isnt fixing us frosty supermilks! Thats why he went and bought a fancy basket a dang apples instead! Hes scared!

Boy, you know I want to say that right to his fat face. But that wont display any maturity. For Dags sake I got to play it polite. So I take the York Peppermint Pattie outta my boot. Yeah, I snuck it from Walgreen special just for me. I admit it.

Sells for a buck seventeen a pop so cant everybody have one, you know? But to hell with it, I cant think with all this noise, so I show that mint chocolate treat to Robbie and say <Check it. I bet a razor blade would fit inside this bitch perfect if we did it sideways.>

Robbie quits his head smacking and Dag sucks up her sniffles and Midge shuts up her squeaks. It happens fast like that. I hand over the Peppermint Pattie and the three a them look at me all grateful cuz I took a jacked up situation and fixed it. All right, yeah. Yeah. I feel a feeling I havent felt since I found a twenty spot Moms lost. Found that valuable bitch in the couch and I didnt keep it for myself and she hugged me strong. Dang. If I knew Id be feeling this tight for handing over a dang Peppermint Pattie Id be Johnny Appleseeding all our stolen candies across this whole great ass nation, forever and ever.

Dag

Monday and Wednesday and Saturday Dag has piano lessons and todays Saturday so shes got to go. Piano Ladys a trip. She laughs like a donkey. Shes got a haircut Dag calls pageboy but I call fugly. She dresses like a lumberjack and has big glasses and big jugs and a big ass too. Dag told me Piano Ladys a gay ass lesbian and I asked her how she knew that and Dag said she just knew. I disagreed but mainly cuz I was disappointed. Piano Ladys roundabout the same age as Robbie. I thought maybe them two could get together and have them some regular people sex and maybe go to the movies and whatnot.

I met Piano Lady the only time I ever went to Dags crib. How it happened was first me and Dag were chilling at Robbies and Dag was fussing about why the people of Middle Earth didnt take out Mount Doom years ago cuz Rohan and Gondor were pretty much right next door. Its a good question and I was proud a my bitch. I ended up walking her ass home past the dozers cuz the answer took a ton of explaining. See, you have to account for geographical terrain like the Dead Marshes and the Ash Mountains and the Drúadan Forest. Natural locations like that slow your armies down and thats usually when your asses get jumped by wargs and fell beasts and crebain, bad mightyduckers like that.

Before I know it we get to this pleasant ass brick ass house with flowers and a driveway and a mailbox. Used to be public housing like on Red Street and Blue Street but a few years back the dozers rolled up and destructed it and up popped these sweet ass cribs called Pinebluff Glenn Estates. Its like they turned Mordor to Hobbiton! People here have riding mowers and sprinklers. Next door to Dag theres two children playing hockey in their driveway with a sweet net I bet their folks got at Target. Place smells nice too. No pee stink or nothing. Only thing I cant figure is where theyre hiding all their dumpsters.

Dag says bye and walks away real quick but I say hold up I got to take a dump. She looks at me like Im gross and my stupid pale ass face blushed up red as hell. Dang, Jody! Dang! If you got to make up stuff in front of a honey dont make it about taking a dump!

She pauses like shes considering if theres a alley close by where a guy can drop a deuce. She lets me in though and, robocop, that casa was kicking! I scope out this humongous ass TV and speakers taller than me and so much light coming through so many windows I just stand there blinking like a fool. Dag tells me to take off my sneaks and even though thats a weird ass rule Im glad I did cuz the carpets the softest carpet my feet ever experienced. I curl my toes in it deep. Dag points down the hall and says the bathrooms on the left and then off she goes. Place is all quiet. You cant hear anyone talking anywhere. Im double thankful for the soft carpet cuz when I sneak off to spy it gives me super stealth.

Dags fam enjoys the hell out a putting stuff in frames. Some a them are pictures of nature. Like a beautiful waterfall on a beautiful mountain. Respect! Dags fam kicks all kinds a photographical ass! Then I remember when Dag and me bused to Target and how they sell beautiful waterfall pictures to anybody that wants one. It still looks impressive though and if I had the cash Id buy me two beautiful waterfall pictures, one for Moms to bring her peace and one for Robbie to cover up the wall holes where mice have babies.

The rest a the pictures are of fam. Dags moms and pops are attractive as hell. Dags pops is popping a suit like George Clooney. And Moms? Id tap that so hard. Bitch has her eyes big and her lips big and her hair big too like Sandra Bullocks, plus shes wearing a sparkly Academy Award dress that shows some nice tittie. If Dag plans on maturing her bod like that then I need to hurry my ass up and grow least a foot and also do something about my wiener. Tight ass abs are only gonna get a killer like me so far.

Her sister Lotte shows up in just one picture. Its a snap of the whole fam but you can tell right off which person got certified nuts. Lottes about sixteen in the picture and shes pretty banging too except she dont have makeup like her moms or ribbons in her hair like Dag. Lottes hairs frizzed out wild and her eyes look like theyve been punched and shes wearing this gray thing that doesnt have any shape and shes smiling like she knows some terrible information the rest a them dont. Honestly? It creeps me out, especially knowing how later Lotte tried to off herself and thats how come her attractive parents locked her spooky ass in the joint.

If you ask me, thats why Dags folks ride Dag like they do. Now its all up to Dag to do them proud. Piano and tap dance are just the start. Girlfriend goes to school at the crack a dawn to talk crap in a debate group and she stays late to blow a flute in some wack ass band. Shes in a coding club and shes like class vice president too and also shes on some special ass math team that answers questions for extra credit or for fun or I dont even know why.

Its not like Im glad Lotte went mental, but let me drop some truth. If Lotte didnt get her ass locked up, then her folks wouldnt a put all their big hopes on Dag, and then Dag wouldnt a rebelled her ass by going secret klepto and forming a whole different secret fam with me and Midge and I guess Robbie too. And Im real grateful for that! But also Im sympathetical too. Cuz now Dags got to be two daughters at once. I dont have degrees in this like Miss Poole but to me it seems like a good way to mess up Dags brain the same way they messed up Lottes.

Dags crapper is cleaner than any crapper I ever saw. Sink, floor, counter, all of it gleaming. I do need to take a leak but its like I got hypnotized. I get the puffy seat up and my wiener out but I cant make pee. Even the inside a the can is clean. And the water smells good. Like flowers. Just doesnt seem right putting pee in that. I think about the bathroom wall in Robbies crib and how its got this yellow crust of pee splatters thats been building up since his parents left so I squat real close so my pee wont make any splatters. I pee a little bit and after I flush I think about washing my hands in that sparkly sink and drying my hands on them fuzzy towels but nah. Id just mess them up.

When Im done theres piano playing coming from somewhere but the house is a maze. I discover a whole other humongous ass TV and this wall rig with a speaker so you can radio other rooms. The strangest thing is this sound like a blender coming from behind a door. It gets me thinking about supermilk so I open the door and theres this little robot shaped like a pizza zooming across the carpet. Its a vacuum. Freaks me out. If Dags fam has robot vacuums they probably also have security cams so I haul ass out a there and bust through some rooms and theres Dag sitting at a piano longside Piano Lady.

Piano Ladys like <Well, hello there> so I say some polite garbage and she laughs and for a minute both a us are cool. Dag though looks panicked. I guess that means her George Clooney and Sandra Bullocks folks dont know about me and if they come home and find a kid like me in their crib Dags gonna be in a fix. Its all right. I aint offended or nothing. House is too clean anyway. I dont even say bye, I just run out the door so fast Im past the flowers and down the drive and at the mailbox before I notice Im footing around in socks but I cant make myself go back and thats why today, and every single other day since, the only thing Ive got for shoes are these nice blue and silver striped snowboots.

Dear Lotte,

Ding-dong, mail call. Can you feel the difference? It's the absence of prying eyes. Papa declared I was old enough to write you without him and Mama peeking. Uh, yeah? I stuffed Clara Bear McGrumpy in the trash over a year ago? It's not like I couldn't have gotten the Clinic's address online if I wanted. Anyway, you better believe I'm using my own hot little hand to drop this in a mailbox. Mama's the world's worst snoop. As you know.

Yes, your fish are F-I-N-E. I can't believe you're still asking about your fish. You care more about those fish than every person on the planet put together. Yes, Papa got promoted. No, I'm not going to smelt all my trophies into cannonballs(?!). Yes, hooray, I've graduated to an A cup. Yes, I'm wearing makeup, and frankly I don't care if you approve or not. No, no one asks about you anymore. Zilcho, nada. But what do you expect, Lotte? You've been gone forever.

I'm tired of answering questions. If you really cared about the answers, you could get better, come home, and find them out yourself.

Sorry if that was mean. I'm a bitch, ha ha ha. Probably because of the pressure I'm under. At least that's what they tell me. Funny, I don't feel any pressure. Think of all the meetings, rehearsals, and responsibilities you used to have. Now double it: that's my schedule. And you know what? It's easy. You ever wonder why other people are so bad at everything? I can't figure it out. However, I did figure out your trick for making Mama and Papa quit watching so closely. If you do *everything*, you can get away with *anything*.

You know what I'm talking about. You're depressed, not dumb. So I'll answer one more question. Yes, I do visit the neighborhood south of The Glenn. Mama and Papa would wig out if they knew, and I suppose I can't stop you from tattling. But if you do, I'll deny it. Remember which of us is the "crazy" one.

It's not like I'm hurting anyone. That one, single time I mentioned Jody in a letter, Mama demanded his pedigree papers. I haven't mentioned him since. But he lives right over on Yellow Street (the bulldozers aren't quite there yet) and I see him most days. He may not be smart, but he's smart enough not to care that I'm President of Coding Club and have the dance solo in High Voltage. He likes me for me. He's the only one in the world who knows the things that really go on in my head. Well, *you* may have some idea, ha ha ha.

Jody's crafty. I know how you like crafty boys, Lotte. Yesterday he was chopping up a tire with a machete. Why, you might ask? I might ask you back, why not? Chopping up a tire makes about as much sense as twirling around gymnastic bars. He kept cutting himself, but I thought the blood looked good. Jody's short, and blood makes short guys look manlier. When boys get in fist fights at PS 220 I always try to get a front row seat. That's why I like public school. There's heroes here, whereas all Our Lady of Heavenly Blessing had were a bunch of girls who were bad in all the same boring ways. No wonder you went bonkers.

I hope you don't think I like-like Jody. I don't. When he smiles, his lip curls up and you can see a tooth that's turned orange. Whenever I think about kissing him, I imagine that tooth tastes like Cheez Curls.

I don't like-like Robbie either. Robbie's a guy who lets me, Jody, and Jody's foster sister Midge congregate at his house. I might as well tell you he's a full-grown man. The sweet, innocent brains of our parents would shoot out their ears if they knew, ha ha ha. Trust me, Robbie has no dishonorable intentions. Unlike Mr. Homewood the gymnastics coach. Or Mr. Cartwright who I had for Home Room.

Robbie gets it. When he was in high school, he was some sort of big shot. Now he's just a guy with no job. What's great is Robbie's the polar opposite of Mama and Papa and lets me and Jody do anything we want. I might as well tell you everything at this point, sister! Robbie gives us tips on stealing things from stores and gives us beer, cigarettes, sometimes even stronger things when we're feeling low.

None of this is any worse than the things you did on Yellow Street. And Brown Street. And White Street. Yes, Lotte, I know all about it. Just because Mama and Papa treat the topic like the Bubonic Plague doesn't mean there aren't plenty of people on Yellow Street eager to talk about it. Maybe you should be grateful they do. If they didn't, would you still exist?

I'm not convinced you would. You keep repeating the same things in your letters, and not just your fish. Your brain's the opposite of my cup size. It's not developing. It's atrophying.

My point is, I always let you live your life, no matter how bad you bungled it. Now you return the favor by <u>keeping your mouth shut</u>. Robbie's place on Yellow Street is a new planet in a new solar system where I don't have to be Perfect Miss Dagmar. I can just be Dag. Let me enjoy it while I can. Before too long, the bulldozers will destroy Planet Robbie. They keep leveling whole blocks to make room for The Glenn, which keeps spreading like a huge, shiny stain. Kind of like your vomit when the paramedics made you upchuck the pills.

Sincerely,
Dagmar

Love

Todays getting real. Realer than any day previous. Robbies made plans in the past but nothing this heavy. All a us are feeling it. So it doesnt make any a us happy when Dag leaves cuz shes the smartest of all a us. She zippers her shiny red jacket and sucks at her knuckles bloody from drubbing the light switch and says how after piano shes gonna finish up her secret costume and be back for trick or treats.

But Im not sure. Her eyes are all bloodshot from crying, you know? It makes me wonder. Dag weaves through the garbage piles and I yell out <Holla at you later?> but I guess shes too far away cuz she dont say anything back. For some reason I get worried shes gonna come up against Deformo but thats never happened before so thats dumb, and pretty soon me and Robbie and Midget are just standing there without dick to say. Rust blowing off in the wind, getting all in our eyes.

Robbies smoking the saddest little butt. He sighs him a big old sigh and says if we cant use the apples then we got to go back to plan A. I aint even in the mood. I explain to him how Dag faked sick three times this month to work on her costume. Robbie ignores me and says how he has to call his new hookup, he just has to do it. Why wont fat boy shut up and listen to me? I explain how the third time Dag faked sick she used her finger, whipped herself up a big mouth a puke and dropped it, splat, right in the middle of social studies. Thats dedication right there! No way Dags going to let anyone screw up her Halloween! But Robbies still talking soft about how he has to get tough, dial the number, and make the mightyducking call.

Fat boys real nervous though cuz what he does instead is light a second sad little butt off the first and try to discuss how theres too many concussions in the NFL and when I dont answer he starts in about how brass knuckles are the best kind of weapon if you really think about it and I throw shade on that crap too. He smokes like hes starving for it and I keep looking down Yellow Street and then he says something like, dang, Jody, you got it bad for Dag, dont you?

Im like robocop please. But I guess I said it too quick cuz Robbie starts dogging me. He has this tard laugh that goes like <Huh, huh, huh, huh!> and its like nails going into my brain. The smartest thing to do is laugh it off but thats difficult cuz now Robbies laughing at how my face is blushing like a little ass girl. Im about to run the hell home to Moms and her TV but then Robbie bends over and coughs real sick and pitiful. Too many a them sad butts made homeboy weak as hell.

He apologizes and says I dont have any reason for shame. I tell him Im not ashamed a nothing and he tells me to chill cuz hes there to tutor my ignorant ass. That sounds like surefire humiliation if you ask me so I go check on Midget whos on her belly in front a that wilted ass jackolantern. The ground at Robbies crib is a bad place to be cuz a all the mice turds and bacteria so Im ready to chew out Midget before I get close and see what she sees.

The pumpkin is stewing with bugs. Dang, how long I been allowing little sister to poke around that nastiness? Beetles and centipedes and little see through insects all squirming around the soggy orange ass guts and spilling out the smiley face I carved. Midgets real into it and has her hand stuck through one a the eye holes so the bugs can crawl up her arm. Her lips are whispering fast like one of them bugs might be good old DAndre. Dang. Wheres Miss Poole when I need her? I aint qualified for this. Im just a dang kid and Im hungry and Im tired and I cant think good.

Robbies still pestering me if I think Dags fly or not and so I say yeah, yeah, shes all right. Robbie crosses his flab arms and asks me if I know that Dags only a child and Im like step off, fat boy, Im a dang youngster myself, theres nothing illegal about it! I start blushing again so I go like who even said I want Dag stamping my V card? Case you didnt notice, girlfriend doesnt have hardly any titties or nothing.

Robbie looks at me like hes disappointed. Jody, he says, dont you know better than to be saying <titties>? No mature ass man uses the word <titties>. Truth is I havent ever heard that piece a knowledge before. So Im like, for real? Robbie frowns wise like Elrond Lord of Rivendell and tells me the word grown ass men use is <tits> and dang, I do have to admit that sounds highly sophisticated.

When I first knew Robbie he was sexing Little Lamb who he said was his girlfriend though I don't know. You ask me, Little Lamb was punking his ass or stealing off his ass or something nefarious cuz she sure didnt seem to have any liking for fat boy. She vanished from the crib pretty quick and that was too bad cuz I had a load a questions for her about how foxy bitches think. After Little Lamb stopped coming round, Robbie wouldnt talk about her. He wouldnt even admit her ass even existed. You even said the word lamb, you got popped.

So fat boys the last person I want romantic help from but now Im curious what else hes got. I mean, I aint ever even kissed a bitch. Robbie struts his yard proud as hell, rubbing his gut like he thinks its sensual. First thing, he says, if you want to be hitting it with honeys then you have to compliment them constant. Yo, I do that! I explain to Robbie how for example I told Dag shes real expert at thieving. Robbie rubs his forehead and says, no, you got to be complimenting her physicality. Like <You have very pretty eyes> and <Your lips are beautiful> and <You have wonderful tits>. Yeah, that makes sense. I wonder if thats how he scored Little Lamb. I swear I start scanning the junk piles for a pen to write this stuff down!

Robbie explains how after you say compliments you have to impress her with skills. Like if youre skilled at busting heads you finds yourself a chump ass sucker and give him a beat down. Or if youre skilled at hunting then you trap a rabbit and skin it and eat it, and dont forget to give shorty a piece.

Even if youre skilled at some boring ass crap like reading you get your ass to the library and rent a stack of thick ass books and when shortys like <What are we doing tonight?> you go like <Yo, bitch, Im reading!>

I dont have any skills except my throwing stars which I can throw with pinpoint accuracy. Problem is, the last time I threw one was at Gwendolyn and you recall how mad Dag got. So I ask Robbie if I should develop new skills and fat boy surprises me. He shakes his big head so hard his greasy hair flops all around. He says throwing star skills are dope, I just need to focus on fending off dangerous villains instead of trying to impale dogs Dag loves with all her heart.

Listen, I didnt ever think Id be saying this, but Robbies advice is tight. I go up top and fat boy slaps me some skin. His chins are jiggling real pleased too. He says before long all the shorties on the block will be wetting their drawers for me. I dont know why theyd want to do that but I keep that to myself. I guess shorties do pee their pants when they get excited. Seems nasty if you ask me but maybe its sexy when it happens for real.

My Wiener Part 2: The Two Towers

Thats right! Lord of the Rings humor free a charge! Take a sec to appreciate that while I figure out if I even want to discuss this topic. It isnt fun, man. It isnt fun at all walking around super concerned about your wiener. I told you how I measured it to make sure it was bigger than a peanut but that doesnt help much when robocops left and right talk about their meat like its the size a their arms. Even if I throw my four point black ronin and take down a raccoon with rabies and Dag thanks me by dropping her drawers? Dont tell Robbie but Im not even sure I could go through with it. Id be too nervous. How am I supposed to know what girls think about wieners? Moms broke all our mirrors with a hammer so Ive been inspecting my junk at Robbies crib and I dont know, it looks proportional and whatnot but not like what they have in porn. For real, I think I might be deformed like Deformo. Sometimes at night I get thinking about it and my stomach starts hurting and then I get diarrhea and I cant sleep and then I have to skip school and then I get detention. And all cuz a my wiener.

Moms

Every time Dag goes home to Pinebluff Glenn Estates I get jealousy. No sense lying about it. Dags folks might go overboard with her activities but they no doubt give her plenty of food and clothes and special gifts. But Moms? You probably figured out Moms had some mental problems a while back. I wasnt hardly old enough to dress myself when she quit cooking and cleaning and going to work and instead started watching TV.

Changes that big dont happen overnight. It happens gradual. One day I was like, Moms, how about you do up some mac and cheese and orange pop like we always do? A hour later, theres no mac, theres no cheese, theres no orange pop, and theres no Moms either. I found her ass flat on her bed and I was like <Whats up?> but all she did was turn up the TV. All right, if Moms needs a day off, thats cool. But then the whole situation of not having food jumped from like a couple days a week to like four days a week and pretty soon it was just the way things were.

Believe, yo, I told her a hundred times how we could get disability funds if we bused our asses to the doc just once and explained how she couldnt get herself out of bed. But Moms was afraid to miss her shows. She seemed for real too.

Meantime our cash was zeroing out so fast I was nightmaring about cooking alley rats for supper and eating our own toes, all sorts a horror movie fates.

I dont know if she saw a commercial or what but thats when she got the idea of fostering. And I got to admit it worked. Moms asked for the worst off child they had cuz they pay the best, so I expected us to get a special ed kid with a helmet. Instead they gave us Midget. Now we pull one large a month for that quiet little bitch! Plus special bonuses like two fifty a year for clothing type junk, one fifty for school junk, forty for birthday junk, and thirty for Christmas junk. Moms even negotiated fifty a month for what she calls diaper allowance and thats a straight up lie. Midget dont need any diapers. Shes peed her drawers three, four times tops.

Dollars add up. We arent living large. But the three a us are surviving. Moms pays her TV bill and doesnt give Midge any hassle. Its not like she dislikes Midge or nothing. She just, you know, trusts little sister to hang with me and whisper to her bugs and all that. Before you get upset about it, let me remind you its preferential treatment compared to DAndres foster mom and all the other foster folks that probably treated Midge weird.

So me and Midge do our thing and Moms views the same shows like shes studying for a test. Give me five bucks and Ill sing you the theme songs start to finish. Dr Phil, The View, Maury. Moms watches so many episodes she hallucinates them. Like when shes viewing Price is Right I hear her answer questions nobody asked, like she goes <Thank you, Drew, you look very handsome yourself!> Thats all right cuz I guess Imaginary Drew Carey says nice stuff to her. But Judge Mathis, hes a mean ass bulldog that says stuff that makes Moms cry. And even Judge Mathis isnt as bad as Mario Lopez. Mario Lopez is this Extra TV mightyducker that talks so cold blooded to Moms that she just screams and screams. Too bad hes not real, otherwise Id jack him up. Instead me and Midge cover our ears and hope Moms turns the channel.

Hearing emotions come out a Moms room all day makes my brain itch so bad I cant deal and thats how my abs got so tight. Dag stole some mags from Walgreen and one had a story called Look Great Shirtless and it turned out to be the magical thing to help my itch. What I learned is you have to Flatten, Shape, and Strengthen if you want a Lean, Hard Waist and Six Pack Abs. That sounded all right so while Moms was doing her TV I started doing the Reverse Wood Chop and Half Seated Leg Circle and Prone Cobra and Rock n Roll Core and Side Jackknife and Oblique Side Bend and at first it wiped me out good. After a time I was repping so hard I only let up during commercials. Thats the best time to rest anyhow cuz Moms doesnt cry or scream or nothing during commercials and if I imagine real hard its like were living in Pinebluff Glenn Estates.

The only time I go inside Moms room these days is for Ellen. We love that dancing bitch. I lay out on the bed with my abs burning cuz a how I been obliterating my fat and I laugh like

Im insane. Moms puts her hand on my back and I can tell shes laughing too. We have us a real nice time but one hour is all I can stand. That room stinks foul. Smells like rotten fruit and bandaids. In January Moms made it all the way to the kitchen to fix back to school toast but she didnt do her robe up good and I peeped a bunch a sores up the insides a her legs. Couldnt eat for crap after that. Put sugar on my toast and gave it to Midge.

Some nights I wake up from bad dreams that whatever disease Moms got is going to get me too. When its the dang middle of the night Im no good at thinking positive. Positive things like how kick ass my pops must have been to make a killer like me. You know he wasnt stuck lying on no bed. He got up, got in his styling suit and his styling car, and got to saving the world. In the middle of the night all I know for sure is I come from Moms. I come from Moms and around here that aint gonna be enough to cut it.

But hold up. Hold up. Dont go thinking critical. Moms surprises me sometimes. Like with the pumpkin. Who woulda thunk Moms would get me a Halloween pumpkin? That right theres enough to give me hope. Give me crazy hope. Barack Obama hope. In fact I take back how I said the shriveled up jackolantern reminds me a Moms. I shouldnta said that. Moms isnt a pumpkin. Theres no bugs spoiling inside her. Shes all right. Shes fine. Believe, yo. One a these days shes gonna turn sharkweek around.

Phone Call

Cuz Robbie gave me free sexual advice I start being supportive about calling up the dealer man. Im like, yeah, boy, youre a righteous hustler and you need to set us up proper for trick or treats! It inspirations him pretty good. Robbie flicks his sad little butt and frowns hard like hes a thug. He starts bouncing on his toes and smacking himself on the head and growling <Mightyduck it! Mightyduck it!> except he aint saying <mightyduck> but thats okay cuz its Robbies crib.

When his face is real red and he looks ready to tear a bitch in two he turns around and swaggers inside with his gut flabbing thisaway and that. Im right behind him but I stop cuz I notice a pair a dope ass gloves poking out under the shell of a busted old hot tub. Hell yes! If I scissors the fingers off these bitches theyll be just like Grishnákh gloves! When Dag sees that shes gonna wet her pants or whatever girls do!

Midget doesnt want to abandon her pumpkin bugs but the weathers getting chilly and sisters gonna get pneumonia if she dont watch it. She knows I mean business so she busts out a roll a duck tape. Where did little sister acquire a roll a duck tape? Anyway she busts out the duck tape and duck tapes the pumpkins eyes and mouth and head hole shut to keep her bug besties safe inside. Well, all right. I guess thats okay if thats her trip.

We go in and Robbies back on his pullup bar trying to bang out a single up. Like I said, thats some comical behavior but this time I keep my mouth shut. I also keep my mouth shut when he leaps to the ground like a Marvel Avenger and does a couple a the saddest pushups I ever saw. Robbie bounces up and while hes all sweaty and adrenalined he grabs his phone and punches in a number and squashes it up to his sweaty ass cheek.

The phone call goes rough. The dumb exercises might a boosted fat boys confidence but they also made him out of breath. Dealer man picks up and Robbies wheezing. Its painful to watch. Robbie goes like <Oh, uh, hello, uh, this is Robbie?> like he aint even totally sure on that fact. I hear dealer man go <Who the mightyduck is Robbie?> and then fat boy has to clear his throat and introduce his dang self like its the first day a school.

Ive learned all kinds a lessons on how you order your drugs. You got to keep it simple. Who you are. What you require. Where you got to go to get it. Robbie behaves like hes trying to ask dealer man on a date. Dudes just rambling. <So, how have you been? Do you still have that El Camino? Anyway, things are going great for me. Ive got a nice place over on Yellow Street. Are you enjoying this cool weather? I sure am. Its my favorite time of year.>

Robocop, what? This a nuclear disaster! My moms is probably embarrassed by now and shes a mile away! Im about to break a thumb motioning for Robbie to end the call before dealer man has all our asses capped just on principle! But Robbie keeps blabbing and pouring sweat and peeling Barenaked Ladies off his hairless titties. Sorry, tits.

Takes like ten minutes of this torture but Robbie does get dealer man to remember who he is. And dealer man laughs! I dont know how these fools know each other but Robbies stuttering like hes one a them speech labbers at school. Then he takes his wackness to the next level. He tells dealer man how he doesnt currently have a ride and does dealer man mind driving the shipment by the house? What! Robbie! Dealer man isnt a Dominos! Robbies the most inept drug purchaser that ever lived!

It is not pretty, yo. Dealer man freaks. Robbie doesnt even stand his ground, he apologizes like a bitch and the end result is he agrees to bus his big fat stupid ass over there and pick up the package his dang self. Now check this. Dealer man hangs up, right? Any dumb ass can see the screen go black on Robbies phone. Robbie, though, he pretends like hes still talking! <Well, all right, that sounds great. Ill see you this afternoon. Goodbye for now.>

Why do I got to always notice stuff like that? Now my nice normal rage at Robbie switches over to feeling bad for his pitiful ass. Robbie grins this big fake ass grin and so I have to grin him a fake ass grin back and both a us know the whole things a bunch of fake ass bull but now both a us are committed to it. Doesnt that make me the same kind a pussy Robbie is? Or worse? I dont know, man, its a real puzzling dilemma.

Robbie claps his hands and announces real loud that supermilk is back on the menu. Midget hears that and her eyes bug and she checks with me to see if its true, if all a us are gonna get our supermilks at last. What do you expect me to say? Im her brother and shes hopping around in her dirty green sweaties looking hopeful as hell and showing me her gap ass missing teeth. So, yeah, I nod my head. Sure, little sister, everyones getting supermilks, that event is definitely occurring. Midge wiggles her butt all excited and I give Robbie a hard look, real hard, the hardest I got, cuz Im not gonna let him disappoint little sister anymore. Not today. Not on her Halloween. You feel me?

Phone Call 2

Midgets so excited she does a dance. She dances her ass around the whole trash ass crib. She doesnt even notice when Robbies phone starts to buzz. Fat boys face goes sick and he probably skids his drawers. I cant figure it. Robbie didnt act like a chump with his last dealer. But this dealer man has his fat ass shook. I half expect Robbie to pick up one a them expensive apples and smash the phone till its dead. Instead he whines <Why wont he leave me alone?> like its dealer man that called him for a package instead a verse visa.

Proud a Robbie, though. He bears down and answers, he goes <Yeah, what?> and then his eyes go big like hes been punked and he sits his wide butt on the table right on top a the apples and razor blades and candies. He responds all perplexed. <Mrs Fullerton?>

Back in the day when Moms was normal, she used to say some things are horses of a different color. Its a saying old folks say that means some sharkweek is different than other sharkweek. Well this horse here is colored different as hell. There isnt nobody in the whole world that gives a mightyduck about Robbie except this one nice old uppity up called Mrs Fullerton. Mrs F has a son and when Robbie was just a child he saved that sons life.

Once there was this football game, right? Folks around these parts are stone cold nuts about high school football. Home team is named the Knights and what folks like to do is come to the games dressed up in armor. Right next to the field theres this hill down where kids go during the game to get high and Robbie, hes just ten years old, he goes there and rolls up on some big teenage fools messing with a tiny little white boy. Their armor and helmets are cardboard like usual but the relevant thing to the story is how their sword isnt a prop. Its a genuine ass sword. Nobody knows where they snagged a real sword but thats not relevant to the story.

Robbie hides his ass before they find his ass. Fools a course keep playing rough with that unfortunate ass child and sure enough things turn accidental and the sword goes right through the side of his neck. You know the perpetrators fled that scene quick. But Robbie crawls his young ass out and investigates. Situations dire as hell. Child is jiggling around, squirting blood as tall as Robbie. If you saw Lord of the Rings you know what kind a damage a sword can do. Even if its not a legendary sword like Glamdring or Andúril. Even if its just some regular orc sword. The Fullerton child is bleeding out and there isnt a single pothead or junkie juvenile around to help.

So Robbie takes off his shirt and wraps it around the childs neck and does it careful without strangulation. Then he picks that child up. My brain cant even cope. But Robbie picks up that bleeding child and climbs up that steep hill and makes it to the Knights field where theres always a ambulance waiting for footballers to break their legs. That Fullerton child poured blood like a keg but he lived, man, he lived.

First time Robbie told me that story, fat boy was proud. Dang straight! If I pulled that Superman stunt off Id be telling my peeps about it every morning noon and night! Robocops would start showing me respect and shorties would be fighting for my wiener. Crossing all those yard lines with that child in his arms was the greatest moment in Robbies whole life. Picture in the paper and everything. But Robbie? Robbies the most confounding adult person I know. These days he doesnt like to speak on it. You bring it up, he hits you.

Course I developed a theory. Mrs F, see, shes kept up with Robbie across all a his miserable ass years. She calls him on the last day of every month plus she sends birthday money and holiday cards and sometimes drops by with angel food cake or pasta salad. Middle school she did it, high school she did it, after Robbie dropped out she did it, and she does it now even though Robbies a grown ass man. That nice old bitch is dependable as hell! So heres my theory. Mrs F reminds Robbie about times he dont want to be reminded of. Every time he gets a phone call or birthday card or pasta salad, more time has gone between him being a young ass hero and him being a fat ass loser thats got cannibal mice in his walls.

I met Mrs F back when I first knew Robbie. Lady brought us a strawberry pie so good I strawberry puked after me and Robbie feasted the whole thing. Mrs F has long brown hair with a gray streak like a garter snake and little round glasses that make her look smart, and the first time she talked to me I was shy as hell. I was all <Yes maam> and <No maam> and my feet kept shuffling like I was a poopypants baby, just like Robbie said. Thats why I feel fat boy on this one. Nice folk like the Fullertons? They dont need to be seeing Robbie while hes spoiling away like meat in a dumpster.

Im mostly psyched it isnt the dealer man calling back to grief Robbie. Midget hasnt stopped dancing for supermilk so I join her clowning ass and we kick through the takeout boxes Robbie uses for plates and big gulps he uses for ashtrays and dried up medicated pads he uses for hemorrhoids and we dont even care about the mice running scared all over. In the kitchen Robbie mumbles the same crap he always does to Mrs F, <Uh huh> and <Nuh uh> and <I guess>, so I get inspirationed and tell Midget what we oughta do is make sure the doorbell works before all them trick or treaters come over to ring it.

We hurry our asses outside and ring the bell but, you know, we got to be inside to hear it, so we haul ass back inside but we go too slow so we run our asses back out and ring it again and this time are ready so we sprint inside hard as hell but still cant tell if the ring is ringing full force so we do the whole thing again and again till we get laughing so hard we belong in the lockup with Lotte. Midges so silly she takes a break to bust out some more excellent headstands on the lawn but sometimes I get in a mood where I go outta my dang head, so I keep going, ringing and running, ringing and running.

Robbie fixes me with a murder look so I know the doorbells got him bugging but I keep at it. Im not deaf. I can hear the call with Mrs F turn bad, and talks dont ever go bad with a nice old bitch like Mrs F. But like I said this day is realer than any day previous, just like tonights gonna be realer than any Halloween ever before, and every time I run past Robbie I hear him say cold robocop crap like <I dont want you calling me anymore, Mrs F> and <Listen to me, youre not welcome here.> Stuff that might break your heart if you werent running around like youre racing the devil.

Punch

Fat boy hits hard. I must a been out ringing the doorbell the millionth time when he hanged up on Mrs F cuz Im zooming by the kitchen when he cement trucks me. Boom, Im buried in trash with my face smushed to a paper plate that smells like burrito. Robbies got me pinned and is whaling. Hitting real heavy across my back and kidneys. Dang, robocop, dang. Ill be pissing pink after this. He cracks a punch to the back a my head and my nose explodes and now Im tasting blood. No, man. You dont do that to your people. So I start hollering how Robbies a retard dicksuck that squats to pee and that he best get off my back unless he wants to get got.

Cuz Im a wily little guy I get myself turned rightside even under all that flab. Dude looks scary. His faces purpler than when he does his worthless ass pullups. Veins pushing out his forehead. Hair stuck to his face like hes half zebra. Roaring nonsense how he aint got time for a white trash fake ass robocop little bitch like me.

He doesnt punch my face. Maybe hes afraid a the pinkeye. Instead he goes at my ribs. I wrap up with my arms best I can and wait it out while these long strings of slobber keep hitting my face. Fat boys spit is boiling. I start kicking and pretty soon I shovel my ass backward through the trash to safety and Im glaring cold at Robbie and Robbies glaring cold at me and we both are panting and nothing happens for a time except some wrong ass clock chiming that its some dang o clock that it aint.

Midgets standing there watching with leaves in her hair from all her excellent outdoor headstands. Its the nose blood thats got her spooked. So I peel a sock off the floor all stiff with I dont even want to know and wipe the blood and the spit and maybe some stupid ass tears too cuz Midgets a kid, she doesnt need to see her brother carrying on like a pussy.

Want to hear the stupidest part? I aint even mad at Robbie. Robbies just some sad ass fat ass thats got issues. The one Im mad at is Mrs F. Every time that uppity up calls she gets Robbie riled. Todays the thirty first and I shoulda knew her call was coming. Im pissed at her irregardless. This is the worst day in human history for Mrs F to be talking her happy crap to Robbie, the day hes invented a honest to god plan and is carrying that plan out with maturity even if it means interacting with people he doesnt enjoy, like for example his new dealer. What Robbies being is a man. You know? Mrs F dont got no cause to squash him back down to a child.

A Letter To My Lawyer Brendan M. Mantle To Show The Judge

To begin with, Judge Your Honor sir this is an Official Letter to my lawyer Brendan M. Mantle who told me to write it bc I'm poor at talking in person bc I "get nervous" & "get frustrated" & "clam up." I also "get nervous" & "get frustrated" when I write things out but I don't "clam up" bc no one's staring at me waiting for me to mess up. Mr. Mantle says this letter might prove I'm a person with Kindness & Intelligence & if you're reading this Judge please know I have those qualities although I didn't quite graduate. Right at the end I got stopped by the Violence which you know about in tragic detail.

(Mr. Mantle like I told you I have a Very Bad habit of writing "bc" & "&" but if I try to change it I "get frustrated" so if you are re-typing this letter can you turn the "bc"s & "&"s into real words? Thank you.)

With this in mind, I want to say right off what I tried to say in the 1st Hearing & which made everyone angry bc I wasn't supposed to talk & that's how over the last few months I've matured into an expert Fixer like my Dad. Last week I fixed a medical model of a lady's sexual privates like you're looking right into a cut open woman. It had cracked plastic but I sawed off some extra Labia Majora on the bottom that you couldn't hardly see & sanded it & welded it over the Uterus. (Mr. Mantle delete this part if it is inappropriate or gross!!!) I also fixed a steering wheel (no car though) & a pipe rack (for if you have a ton of pipes) & a log carrier (a thing for carrying logs). It's true none of this was for money but I hope you'll agree it means my future as a Fixer is Bright.

Correspondingly, Judge Your Honor sir you made it Very Clear I need to have a job before I show my Disrespectful Face in your court again & I've been trying so hard & to be perfectly honest totally failed. I was going to do a thing nailing roofs but I missed the interview & Judge sir I know you're thinking What Is Wrong With This Kid but it wasn't my fault. If you can believe ~~this shit~~ (Mr. Mantle I crossed it out but please delete the word "shit" completely!!!) it there was a Gun Shooting & ~~pigs~~ ~~fuzz~~ (Mr. Mantle you know what to do) police officers weren't letting folks on Yellow Street leave their homes.

Moreover, I had a Very Positive job interview to rip apart computers & phones with a lady boss who said I was "Very Sweet" until she looked at my Record & figured out who I was & said she would be "Highly Uncomfortable" with me working there & even dialed 9 & 1 when I tried & tried to make her understand how bad I needed that job bc of what you said Judge. You could call it yelling technically but I was only trying to be Firm & I don't agree security guards were necessary.

Additionally, I want to be Honest with you Judge Your

Honor sir bc like Mr. Mantle said being honest is the 1st step in processing the grievances of people I've hurt emotionally & physically. But the truth is Judge sir & it may sound selfish but I can't get a fair shake in this ~~goddamn~~ town! (Mr. Mantle.) On my side of town everyone knows what I did bc as you know about 300 people saw it happen & there's videos & I wish I would've gotten that job ripping up computers & phones bc maybe I could've destroyed some of those videos forever. I wanted a McDonald's job form & the girl said she'd throw fry grease in my face unless I vacated the premises. Judge this is a Free Country & I just wanted a Quarter Pounder & this is a Threat to an American so why don't you arrest her & not me? (Mr. Mantle is this OK???)

Significantly, I want to show you Judge Your Honor sir my Scrapbook. (Mr. Mantle have you changed your mind about this???) I Really want to show you it. (Mr. Mantle please don't delete this part!!!) My Mom made it & I know you're thinking of course the Defendent's mom is going to say nice things about her delinquent son but remember Judge I got LEFT BEHIND by my Mom & Dad who never say anything nice about me so this Scrapbook is unbiased empirical proof (Mr. Mantle right words???) of my Kindness & Intelligence. When you read it Judge sir it's my belief you will Enter It Into Evidence & be personally Touched to see a Young Man with a lot of Promise.

Markedly, I know I ruined my future with Violence but think of that plastic Uterus I fixed & imagine it's my Mom's Uterus & what if you Judge sir had the power to weld me back inside there so I was born different & better? That's what Mr. Mantle calls a "Thought Experiment" & I know it's weird but I Really Really don't want to be tried as an Adult & go to prison & don't even want to go to juvie bc I think I will do Very Poorly there too.

To be sure, Judge sir all I want is to run away & please don't panic & send a bounty hunter bc I won't actually do it although I think about it every minute. Everyone used to say I was a slam dunk to get a full athletic scholarship including tuition & a room & books & food but I never cared about any of that bc all I wanted was to Get Out of this town & scrub it off me until I scrubbed off all the old Robbie too & the guy left over was shiny and clean like the baby pictures in my Scrapbook.

Forthwith, yes Judge Your Honor sir I've been Using & I don't care if Mr. Mantle doesn't want me to say it (Delete this if you want Mr. Mantle but I'm trying to Open My Heart!!!) bc Mr. Mantle's the one who said I can't fix anything until I can be Honest. I have huffed freon & done a speedball & did some GHB & smoked tons of low quality pot. I know Judge sir this doesn't matter but I didn't enjoy any of it & so might as well quit Using forever bc what's the point if you can't enjoy it?

Notwithstanding, I'm ready to admit I stole Many Items (Mr. Mantle I respect you & am glad you're my Lawyer but can't you feel the Value of saying this?) from the Walgreen's close to my home on Yellow Street after I was LEFT BEHIND by Mom & Dad & even though I'm not even 20 I'm living as an independent man & making my own way in the world & if that means I have to steal some trail mix or T.P. or shaving blades don't you think that's a Minor Offense on a street where people sell drugs & pimp bitches all the time? I'll make it up to Walgreen's Judge sir, I'll do anything you say, I'll wash bum puke off the Walgreen's sidewalk or dress up like a Salvation Army Santa, just don't Throw The Baby Out With The Bath Water as Mom used to say. In this Thought Experiment I'm the baby.

You know really I don't care anymore Judge sir bc as long as I'm on a roll why not be Honest about Every Fucking Little Thing? (Mr. Mantle, I don't give a shit!!!) All these big words I'm starting paragraphs with are stolen too from a worksheet my teacher Mr. Toppen titled Examples of Transitional Phrases which I found by my Scrapbook. Mr. Toppen told us you should start all your paragraphs with Transitional Phrases if you want to sound Educated so Judge sir I confess to the Court that's what I'm trying to do & I could've kept going bc there's a million of these phrases such as By The Same Token & Henceforth & Be That As It May & Conversely but instead I choose honesty & I throw myself on the Mercy Of The Court.

Yes I destroyed someone's life with violence. Yes I did. But I'm trying & will keep trying & maybe someday can help others who are also trying & need help to make better Choices & even maybe Youngsters who have been through things Even Worse than me & I can help by being a friend & that's worth something isn't it? Maybe I can be a different kind of Fixer & fix their troubles like I fixed the Uterus & maybe when I'm done fix my own stupid self too. Thank you for your time Judge.

Robbie

Let me tell you a secret. I know why Robbies rageful. I know why he hates this town and I know why tonight he wants to mightyduck it up. Fat boy was high as hell one night and he told me the whole sad story. He didnt tell Dag and he didnt tell Midget. This is the kind a thing you keep strictly between robocops.

A long time after he was a newspaper hero Robbie turned himself into a Knight. He was footballing fierce from the day he started middle school. Robbie says he wasnt fat back then and I believe it cuz you cant be dodging tackles if youre humping around a extra hundred. Every time fat boy hit the field he owned it. Dude was kamikaze. Leaping right over the line. Taking a pass across what he calls the midfield. Win or lose, didnt matter. Robbie laid his body out. Pretty soon bleacher bums start chanting his name and fly cheerleaders start putting special posters on his locker. Boy was living large.

I havent myself been on any sports teams personally but I know theres hardly no freshmen that go straight to varsity. But thats what happened. Ninth grade and pow. My boys a baller. Butting helmets with king kongs but hes hanging. Getting himself tattooed regular, but hes hanging. Coach S puts a quote in the paper how Robbies got raw talent like hes never seen and thats a badge a honor cuz in this town people respect Coach S better than Jesus. But Coach S also says raw talents not enough and if you want to be a starter at fourteen you got to work twice as hard. So what Coach S does is line up this assistant coach to work with Robbie special after practice.

You know how teachers are always blabbing on sex abuse like its their favorite thing to blab on? And how all the books the school librarian wants us to read has kids gaining important lessons about sex abuse? Well that boring ass school library junk actually happened for real to Robbie! Hes all sex abused and whatnot and its not boring after all. Ninth grades hardly even started for fat boy when that assistant coach I mentioned starts pulling some serious afterhours unethics.

Robbie laughed like it was funny when he described it and I went along and laughed too cuz I was enjoying a supermilk and its nice when Robbies in a positive mood. But, yo, for real? That sharkweek was mightyducked. Robbie said the dude didnt even touch his wiener. What he did was put his thumb up Robbies butthole. Dont ask me why. It was just his thing. He stuck it up there and with his other hand he sexually enjoyed himself or however you want to put it. What Robbie told me super secret was that he didnt hate it that much. Didnt hate the assistant coach either. He was just scared someone might walk in and witness it, cuz if that news got out the situation round school would get rough.

What Robbie calculated was if the thumb stuff was part a his extra practice, then he just had to get so skilled he didnt need any extra practice. Hard to believe even Robbie was that dumb but thats how he thunk it out. So homeboy OGd that sport. He clocked defense boys so hard their helmets flew off. He dove with the ball like he was trying to break his neck. Other teams accused him a roiding up but he peed clean. Plus hes touchdowning like a pimp so whats Coach S gonna do? Bench his freshman ass?

Meanwhile hes getting banged up. Hes puking buckets on the sidelines and fainting when he comes off the field and at school hes having headaches so big hes crying tears. Robbie asks me if I know what all that signifies and I say do I look like a medical doctor? So he tells it to me straight. Concussions. Concussions like crazy and his coaches didnt see fit to do a thing. So Robbie keeps running and jumping and puking and fainting cuz, you know, he prefers not having a thumb up his butt every night before supper.

The seasons about over and Robbies chilling in biology. The biology teacher gives the whole class sharp ass pins so they can learn their blood type which sounds revolting if you ask me, but I guess thats the kind of stuff teachers did back in medieval times. Robbies prepping to blood himself when the teacher gets a note that says Robbies got to get with Coach S. Every single biology pimp and biology ho quits poking their fingers cuz this news is flabbergasting. No kid in history ever got a private daytime conference with Coach S.

So Coach S is this handsome blond hustler thats cut even though hes old. Dude pounds so much coffee hes got two pots blasting twenty four seven and his whole body vibrates like he wants to pitbull your throat. Ask any footballer and theyll tell you if you find yourself in Coach Ss office you better be ready to sweat it out. Thats how Robbie can tell things arent normal. Coach S isnt yelling. Hes smiling and offering Robbie a chair and a thing a coffee. Robbie takes the chair but not the coffee cuz Robbies got good taste like me and knows coffee is some foul ass dirt tasting garbage.

Coach S found out about the butthole deal. He doesnt mention if he learned it from a spy or secret camera or what but he apologizes. Robbie tells me its real obvious Coach S isnt used to saying sorry. Dude pounds coffee every other word and fidgets like he needs to drain a leg. He explains how hes gonna deal with the assistant coach private and he doesnt see a reason anyone has to know about this, and also by the way Robbies fixing to make all state if he keeps going strong on the field. Coach S is being all complimentary and reassuring and muscular. Hows Robbie supposed to react to that? Hes not even grown.

So check this out. Nobody calls the popo. Nobody gets fired. Next season comes and the assistant coach is steady working and Coach S is acting like nobodys thumbs ever been up nobodys butthole. That gets Robbie feeling strange, I guess, so he just tries to focus real hard. He miracles that football in the end zone a hundred thousand times. Sophomore year, junior year, senior year. Meanwhile sets a Guinness record for concussions. Knights are winning, though, so nobody cares how, not in this evil ass town they dont.

But privately and whatnot? Fat boys building a Eiffel Tower a rage. Hes the danged star of the danged team but he still aint got any dang friends? Still cant score a single piece a ass?

I wasnt there but Ill tell you this. Females are good at sensing things with their instincts. No doubt all the cheerleaders and girlies intuitioned Robbie wasnt normal. Robbie even told me straight up, after he got buttholed he wasnt even sure about his sex stuff until Little Lamb.

Man, I dont know. Thats a lot of heavy stuff to be blaming on a thumb up your butt. Dont tell anybody but I put a thumb up my own butt just to check it out and I guess it was weird but I sure didnt lose my dang mind over it.

Anyway Robbie focused his rage on Coach S. If youre from around here I dont have to tell you how it went down. It was climactic as hell. Last game a the year. Clock running out and all that. Knights got to win or they miss the playoffs and around these parts thats worse than 9/11. And Robbie does what he always does. He busts out with the ball like a robocop on fire. Nobodys got the ability to stop his powerful ass. Crowds jumping. Cheerleader tits bouncing. Player is in full effect. The kind a stuff you dream about. Robbie never crossed that field so victorious since he carried Mrs Fs little boy to safety.

Nobody in the world knows why Robbie did what he did except me. Robbie blended me another supermilk and told me exclusive. He was hauling ass down the sideline to win the game and he happened to pass Coach S and Coach S wasnt cheering or clapping or nothing. He was smirking like he owned Robbies ass. That filled Robbie with feelings, you know? Like his ass had been played by grown men that oughta know better and all this cheering was for selfish ass adult mightyduckers that looked the other way.

Robbie stops right on the one yard line. Id give my left nut to see a video of that. Homes just pulls up short. Coach S is making noise now, right? Hes jumping and spitting like hes having a epileptical. Robbie turns around so cold the other team just backs off. Players are standing all confused and the refs are whistling their whistles and just like that the Knights whole season is junked but Robbie doesnt care, hes walking then jogging then sprinting full force at the bench and before anyone knows whats up fat boy takes out Coach S with the baddest hit anybodys seen all game. Robbies life is full of wack ass stuff but that hit? He can stand tall on that forever.

Takes like ten players to stop Robbie bashing. A while back I met this Mexican working the corner across from school, goes by the name a Speck, and Speck says he was sitting in the front row chomping a chili cheese dog when that legendary occurrence occured, and he says Coach Ss face was like a plate of blood and teeth. They ambulanced that big blond bastard out a there quick but it was too late cuz he was messed up big time.

Speck said he scoped out Coach S at Hardees a couple years later and he wasnt handsome any more and Speck only knew him cuz a his Knights sweatie. His nose jacked as hell and one eye wonked way to the left. Nastiest of all was his mouth cuz the top jaw dont meet up correct anymore, not even after they wired the pieces back together. Supposedly Coach S had to smoosh his fries with a plastic fork before he pasted the potato paste between his big giant replacement teeth. Hardees people came by and gave him respect but he threw a napkin holder at them.

The end a that game was game over for Robbie too. Might as well have raped Santa Claus. He was underage and his lawyer was all right so he did juvie instead a the clink but I think it was still pretty rough. Course I asked him if he ever told anybody the truth about what went down and Robbie didnt answer but I bet if he did spill it, it landed soft, you know what Im saying? Besides you cant have molester junk talked about on the streets and expect to have any peace.

While Robbie was in juvie, people went wild on his parents crib. At some point I guess his folks had enough of all the spray paint wieners and cat death and fire bottles and trucked their asses out. Did it fast too. Left all their nice junk, all the incredible clocks, not to mention the whole actual physical house. Problem is, a house stills got bills. And Robbie was just a dumb juvenile. Theres wasnt a whole lot a job prospecting for the boy that did Coach S, you know? Even them that did hire Robbie ended up firing his ass, cuz Robbies brain has problems from all those years a concussions.

Robbie has a library card. Yeah, it surprised me too. One day he bused his fat ass there and computered till he got a page describing how concussions mess you up. Dag had to read it out loud cuz Robbie says white paper blinds his eyes. I know that sounds made up but it turns out its one a the symptoms! It said so right on the page! Dag read the whole thing and dang if it didnt describe Robbie perfect. It said how concussioned people cant focus and overreact about everything and cant sleep proper either. They get worried and depressed and emotional and mad, and when they get older like Robbie they get dementia.

Robbie goes <Im officially crazy, I guess.>

Hate to say it but I agree. Least it explains why Robbie has so many stupid behaviors. Back in school he chilled at this place The Lung, where if you was a athlete you could play pool and darts and smoke up and drink lots and the owners just laughed and said what a good game you boys played. Couple years after he attacked Coach S, brain damaged Robbie went back to The Lung, I guess cuz he was lonely and thought bygones were bygone, and he told me he got the worst beating he ever got. He coughed up gunk for a month.

The most maniacal mightyducker was this boy Ketchum, #69 back when he played with Robbie. When I heard that name I cracked how Ketchum better be ketchum some touchdown passes but Robbies never appreciative of puns. Anyway he informed me Ketchum was a offensive guard that worshipped Coach S, so when he saw Robbie in The Lung he didnt waste any time clobbering fat boy in the head with a glass pitcher. Must a been a miracle pitcher from god cuz it didnt crack, not even after Ketchum did Robbie with it about fifty times. Ketchum filled that pitcher with beer and last thing Robbie saw before he passed out was his own blood mixed up in beer, swirling around, and #69 slurping it right down his throat.

Back when he used to earn some chip, Robbie got lifted constant, smoking and snorting and philosophing like he was a deep ass dude, and now and then he reflected on The Lung, how later it felt like the whole town was drinking his blood every day. Screwing up his car back when he owned a car. Having hos fake flirt then laugh in his face. Getting his hard working ass fired from every piece a crap job there was. Making fun a how he didnt have any people no more. Just doing him wrong over and over just because he didnt know how to stop getting butt thumbed in a locker room when he was little. So, yeah, robocop. Hes got rage. Hes got it deep. Took him a time but now fat boys ready to step up.

Natural Light

Dag and me were proud about choosing Three Musketeer instead of Snickers but now Im having doubts. Robbie selects some items from what he calls the utility drawer. Tacks and nails and staples and pins. Fat boys getting creative. He snaps off the sharp edge of a thing a packing tape. Practically slices his thumb off while he does it. But when we try getting all the sharp objects inside candy bars? Nope. Three Musketeers too fluffy. Keeps squooshing out like pus. Fat boy pushes this sharp little screw in a Three Musketeer real careful and asks how it looks and I reply honest. It looks like a Three Musketeer with a screw in it!

Robbie has no humor left. Not today. He chucks the delicious candy bar right off my ear, and after I brush off the floor scuzz and dig out the screw I eat it cuz its about noon and I havent had crap for food. Cant enjoy it, though. The first reason is cuz my mouth tastes scabby from when my nose bled down my throat and the second reason is Robbies mad at me and he has a right to be. What did he tell us? He told us Snickers! Snickers! It burns me up when I screw up simple stuff. I need to redeem myself with a brainstorm so I start looking around the kitchen. And guess what? A big ass brainstorm is exactly what I get!

Theres a couple a Natural Light empties on top a the fridge from back when Robbie had the green for bottles instead of cans. Theyre half filled with Robbies old spit from back when he had the green for chaw but I dump that sludge and go smash. I bust the bottles right over the sink. Robbie starts bugging but I tell him to hush.

I use a calendar to transfer a bunch a sharp broken glass bits to the table. Its a calendar Robbies old man had of sexy ladies and Octobers a sexy witch flying a broom and even though its ancient Im glad Robbie keeps it around cuz sexy witches make Halloween even nicer. Next thing I do is look for a object thats got serious pounds to it, like a brick, but the heaviest thing I find is a dented ass can a soup. Robbies groceries are always dented for some reason. I guess hes got bad luck choosing groceries. Anyway I start pounding the glass with the soup on top a the sexy witch. Robbie clues in on my brainstorm and takes over smashing duty cuz even though hes obese hes way stronger than a small ass kid like me.

Now we have a pile of twinkly little grinded up shards. They go slivering into Three Musketeer real smooth and its easy smushing them into Gummy Body Parts and Gummy Bugs. Dag bought two Pez, one with a witch head and one with a pumpkin head, and no nails or pins are gonna fit in those plastic tubes. But a nugget a glass fits perfect. Nicest surprise of all is the Twirl Pops I bought for Midget. If you lick the pops first the grinded up glass sticks to it and looks like sugar and then you can just wrap it back up. Man, can I be honest with you? Im feeling special as hell. That right there was my idea. Nothings ever my idea at school.

Two Natty Lights dont go far though. We make enough for about ten, twelve trick or treaters. Wont last us five minutes when Halloween in the hood gets thick. Robbie keeps eyeing all the clocks even though Midget screwed up the times. But I know what hes thinking. Hes thinking its time to motor his ass across town and get the package. Im glad cuz sooner or later Robbies got to nut up. Plus I think its better if we candy up with drugs instead a glass cuz when I imagine children with blood coming outta their mouths? I dont know. Just dont like to think about it is all.

Before Moms turned serious about TV she taught me it was shameful to create waste so I find a White Castle napkin and scoop the leftover glass dust off the sexy witch into a box of Spooky Nerds. After that I discover Robbie supermodeling in the bathroom mirror. The mirror has all these little dots from when Robbie pops zits. Fat boys put his nice black jacket on top a the Barenaked Ladies. It fits too tight cuz fat boy is fat and makes a fart noise cuz his skin is slick from Total Body Hair Removal. Robbie also busts out a comb and parts his hair and combs out the dandruff too. I take a sec to appreciate all that respectful behavior. Things are rough around the way. No doubt. Robbie, though, hes striving, you know? Hes striving to get things right.

Flypaper

Once hes got his do done, he tells me to round up Midget and make sure she hasnt pooped her drawers or nothing. Im like huh? Why do tiny children need to come along for illegal drug stuff? Me and Midge dont have people on that side of town. We dont even have money for the bus! I tell him straight up this is bull but Robbie fronts hard and says all of us are in this sharkweek together and if we expect to get big frosty supermilks we better learn supermilks dont grow on trees.

Fat boy can do speeches all day but thats not gonna change the sorry ass fact that this combed hair jacket wearing mightyducker is scared a going to pick up his package and hes aiming to protect his cowardly ass with a couple a small ass kids. That heats me up! On the other hand, what I dont need is two fat boy beat downs in the same day. Theres still TP wadded in my nose from the first one.

Midgets been missing for a while now but Im not a Pinebluff Glenn Estates parental making the uniforms do Amber Alerts all day. It dont work like that on Yellow Street. Little sisters probably rutting through junk like a little sister ought to. I check all the best piles but nope. Next I look under the table where Midget likes to sleep cute like a baby kangaroo but nope. Then I check the bathtub where she likes to play naked but nope. Little bitch isnt anywhere. I start working up a sweat before I think a Robbies garage. I bust in and sure enough theres Midge staring way up high.

Back when Robbie was holding road signs, he used the cash to transform his garage into what he called a bachelors den even though he let Dag and Midge and Little Lamb in too. He styled it up like he was an amazing style faggot from TV. He stringed up Christmas lights and found a rug that didnt have hardly any stains. Theres a boom box too that works if you put the Illustrated World Encyclopedia of Guns on the CD door to keep it shut. He painted the walls up neat and in the middle he put a metal table with beautiful flower designs, and in the center he gave a place a honor to a cool ass statue of Stonewall Jackson. Stonewall Jackson was this Civil War dude that had a army that beat the sharkweek outta armies ten times bigger just like in Lord of the Rings. Robbies real into the Civil War cuz he says his full name is Robert Edward and his folks named him that cuz hes a distant relative of Robert E Lee, Stonewall Jacksons boss. Dont ask me if its true. But I hope it is.

Gay TV style faggots taught me how all rooms need a signature piece and I guess Robbies signature piece is this big gold couch he got from the street and bleached for germs. You always got a mess a bug bites when you relaxed on the golden couch but still as signature pieces go its pretty dope. Back in the day? The good old day? Dang, boy. Wasnt any better place in the world to smoke a bowl or huff a bag or slurp a supermilk than Robbies super styling secret bachelor den.

After Little Lamb the garage went nasty. It stinks like Robbie hid a poop. For some reason the floors are covered in dried mud. Also the Christmas lights are busted, every single one, so there isnt any magical feel left. Even the naked girlies Robbie taped up are so yellow and wrinkly theyre zombies compared to the sexy calendar witch and dont have effects on my wiener. Robbies beautiful flower table got wrecked too like somebody hulked out on it, probably Robbie, and thats where Midge is standing, balanced all dangerous on top a pile a twisted up metal. Whole thing makes no sense till I look up and see where Midges looking.

Five strips a flypaper dangle off the ceiling. Flypaper has a fruity ass stink that doesnt stink like anything else. After Moms leg sores showed up, about a thousand flies moved into her room so I traveled my ass to Walgreen and bought flypapers from Dick Trickle but Moms said if I put flypapers up she was gonna vomit cuz flypaper is stone cold barbaric. I feel Moms on that one. Flypapers are unsightly for sure. They come out the tube all bright and yellow but these five in Robbies den for example are all black cuz a how many fly bodies are stuck on. A few a them bitches are still wiggling too. Midget a course is interested as hell, bouncing on tippy toes to get close.

Robbie rolls in quick. Right off hes hollering at Midget to get her ass off the scrap pile but she acts like shes deaf so Robbie runs up and I get nervous cuz Robbies clumsy and what if he makes Midge fall? Life is full a mysterious coincidences cuz thats the exact sec I notice old Stonewalls ceramic head smashed all over the floor. My brain is strange cuz I get two opposite thoughts. How I dont want Midgets head to get busted up like Stonewall and also how Stonewalls busted head parts might squoosh good inside a Three Musketeer.

But Barack Obama hero blood is running through these veins! Before Robbie can get there I put my arms around Midgets legs and lift her off the heap. She still snags three gnarly flypapers like its the most important thing she ever did. Dead ass flies start bouncing across my face and sticky paper is sticking to my lips and it tastes worse than coffee. Im not happy. Im not happy at all. But what else is a big brother supposed to do? I set Midge on the golden couch and she goes zooming inside with her flypapers like she thinks Im plotting to steal them. Meantime Robbies just standing there with his hands on his chest like he barely avoided a heart attack.

He goes <I need to put a lock on this garage. It is not safe for children.>

And Im thinking <Dang, boss, aint anything in this crib safe for children. Why you think we even come here?>

Robbie covers up his fear for safety by bellyaching how late we are, how all a us are gonna piss off dealer man, how the outlooks gonna be bleak if we miss the next bus. But Robbie can eat a dick. Didnt my heroing earn me a single minute for myself? I march my ass in the bathroom. I dont have time to style like a player but at least I got to wipe the nosebleed crust off my face. Robbies sink is foul though. Hair clogs big as dead mice and knobs all scummed with black fungus. Im not looking to get contaminated with Robbies scabies and rabies and herpes and whatnot. Plus is water supposed to be orange?

So instead I go to the toilet and lift off the back lid cuz one time this girl at school educated me how water in the back of a toilet is super clean. I get me a whiff and Im not so sure. Smells ripe to me. But Robbies shouting and I dont have time to be a pussy so I scrub my face in toilet water. Dang, yo. Am I really doing this? At least Dags not here to see! Also I rinse out my pinkeye cuz if any cheeses out in front of dealer man thatd be straight up humiliating.

Fat boys waiting by the front door tapping his foot like a old lady. While Im laughing at that entertaining behavior a cold wind blows up and dead leaves come shooting inside the crib and go twirling all around. I dont know, its sort a pretty. Its like snow. Like Halloween snow. If Dag was here, she might go spinning and dancing in them leaves cuz thats the kind of graceful ass girly stuff she likes to do.

Robbie yells how I got to knock off the daydreaming and get my ass in gear. I guess hes not making Midget come after all cuz shes sitting in the corner chattering to her flypapers like its a little kid tea party. Thats a relief and I dont want Robbie changing his mind on that, so I run for the bus stop fast as Legolas son of Thranduil.

Everybody in Middle Earths son of somebody. Thats how it oughta be. Just think a Robbie. Maybe his folks are gone but he did say he was the great great great great great grandson of an Irish king and also has a aunt whos giving him a caribbean house and also a distant relative of Robert E Lee. Maybe one of them is true. Maybe all of them is true. Makes me wonder who Jodys got. Who Jodys really got. If my Barack Obama pops dont ever show and Moms dont ever get better and Robbie gets his ass hauled off to jail. Maybe Jodys not son of nobody. Im ruminating on this gloomy ass concept when the bus pulls up and both me and Robbie get coughing from exhaust and I realize how not a single one a Robbies clocks were ringing when we left. Yo. Bad omen, man. For real.

Kyle

Time to time I ride the bus to Yellow Street when its icy cold but this route isnt my route and Im not acquainted with these particular crackheads. Whole back a the bus is took up by this white lady that breathes like a pig and is wearing scraps a rags all filthed together. Across the aisle from me is this black brother and hes a straight up junkie with his skin mightyducked and his teeth mightyducked and his eyeballs jerking around like he thinks the whole group a us are gonna pull our knives. Theres also this gal that looks real normal except every five minutes she screams out incredible truth bombs like <ALL MY BANK ACCOUNTS, WHY ARE THEY SHRINKING?> and <THE CHINESE CONTROL THE PRESIDENT!> I dig this bitch! Too bad shes gonna end up playing checkers with Lotte.

Then this dude with no legs gets his wheelchair lifted in with a elevator thing and even though it takes a long time its fascinating cuz I enjoy science. Robbie though hes so impatient he starts hollering at No Legs Man about how hes gonna be No Arms Man too if he doesnt hurry his ass up. Other folks give Robbie applause like they think handicappers are the root of all evil. Violence is thick up in that bitch. I wish I had my Barack Obama mask so I coulda gone to the front all presidential and been like <All us robocops got to chill cuz at the end a the day all a us are Americans and we got to deal with our stupid ass problems together.>

You know Robbies big time stressed cuz he doesnt let me pull the cord for our stop and thats the funnest part. The hood we step out at? First time I ever laid eyes on it. Its got a liquor store and a place for lotto tickets but the rest a the block is boarded up and theres not any folk like, you know, living lives, besides the corner crews signaling the boys across the street to hook up buyers. You know how crack boys do. Also the whole block stinks a fish. I ask a squirrel whats up with that. Cuz theres a squirrel there too.

Fresh turf cant shake me. True, the people here arent demographical like they are in my hood. In my hood theres a lot more white folk that I guess fell on hard times or got IRSed or what have you. I get a bad thought and I mean real bad. What if these pushers think Robbies my pops? Thats a nightmare scenario! If they jack Robbie, then they got to jack me as well. And who doesnt lay eyes on Robbie and want to jack his fat ass?

Robbie scopes the road signs and waddles his butt to a corner where we meet a grade school girl tough as hell. Kid spits expert too, accurate like me and my ninja stars. She talks fast, laying it out about blue tips and yellow stripes and da bomb and how much we want a each. Robbie cant get a word in. After the child finishes she pats her stomach like shes gonna show us her gat unless we speak up. Robbie says hes supposed to get with Kyle so wheres Kyle at? Girl says mightyduck off. Robbies got twenty years on this diaper baby but hes sweating it. He shows her his phone record with Kyles digits. Girl considers it and says if we two are fibbing shes gonna place a cap in both our behinds. Robbie smiles like thats a fair deal. Speak for your dang self, homes!

Little girl passes us off to a tall brother with giant headphones and a mess a scars on his cheek and also no ear, and this tall disfigured music enjoying deaf brother takes us down the way to a pretty nice place with a good fence where he knocks on a door and talks real quiet through the crack before he waves our asses in. Robbie a course has to bust out his church voice. He goes <Thank you very much, I appreciate the assistance.> By now Im practically praying we do get filled with heat.

We stumble our asses down a dark scary hall that has cool colored lights at the end. I dont know what Im expecting. Room full a gold? Bunch of G string shorties rubbing their butts on stripper poles? Well, its nothing like that but its still pretty tight, a big spacious ass room styled so correct its like weve entered a fantasy land. Blue neon lights glowing everywhere and freestyling from the speakers is none other than my boy Lil Wayne. Hey! Thats my joint right there!

Im krumping before I even notice the bar stocked with a thousand alcohols and the walls with a bunch a life size pictures a soccer dudes. I dont know sharkweek about soccer but maybe I oughta learn! Rest a the rooms got foosball and a pool table shaped like a stop sign and wait, wait, hold up. Dang, robocop! This crib has a ferret! Now I wish Midget had come after all cuz little sister enjoys the hell outta wildlife. This bad ass ferret is bopping around to Lil Wayne and is wearing a scarf.

Furniture is tight too. Big pink and yellow bean bags and chairs that look like eggs. Plus theres two pimped out lazyboys facing a projector screen playing Mass Effect the best I ever saw it played. The video game mastermind is this dude wearing a red do rag and doing his controller so fast its like hes got supernatural powers. Id be satisfied to stand here the rest a my life watching this genius do his thing but you know Robbie. Fat boys always got to be crapping the bed.

Robbie introduces himself real formal. Kyle, I guess this is Kyle, he ignores it. Hes got some video game people he needs to slay. After some rad explosions he pauses the game and strolls to the bar to pour him some pistachio nuts. Kyles wearing a whitey like hes street but also PJ pants with palm trees and pineapples. He yawns like massacring all them computer men wiped him out. Oh and check this. Dudes fat. Like Robbie fat. How come his fat makes him look like a cool ass killer?

<Whats wrong with your boy?> Kyle goes.

<Oh, hes just dancing> Robbie says.

Dancing? This is krumping, bitch! Maybe Kyles got a rule about no krumping in the crib and even though thats a bullcrap rule he does have a ferret in a scarf so you got to credit him for that. The neon in the room goes from blue to pink and Kyle sighs huge like hes sick a dealing with dumb asses and their krumping sidekicks. He doesnt even look at us when he does the menu. Doesnt confuse us like the little girl did with brand names either. Sugar, base, stones, caps, horse, bolt, bump, beans, A, E, TNT, dust, crystal, reefer. He rattles off prices too. Not bad for a dude half sleeping.

Robbie does a retard grin and whips out his chip. Yo! You arent supposed to flash cash like that! Kyle starts scanning like we might be narcs. He asks Robbie who I am. Robbie says Im nobody. Kyle asks how come Robbie only has small ass juveniles for friends, he a pervert or something? Robbie says Im not a friend, Im just some kid that keeps showing up to his crib.

Dang. Thats cold. Makes me feel kinda low. Kyle laughs real mean and he goes <Whats wrong with little mans eye?> and Robbie says I have pinkeye and Kyle makes a face like hes disgusted and then he squints so he can read my jean jacket. <Sandwich Gamble, whats that?> Chuckling mightyducker asks it like hes ignorant and now I dont give a sharkweek if hes the baddest Mass Effect player that ever lived, Im gonna set his ass straight. My markering isnt perfect, but its obvious it says <Samwise Gamgee> and Samwise Gamgee happens to be my number one robocop. Before I can say anything Robbie finishes counting and holds out his money.

Kyle shakes his do rag head. Hes all woke up now. He says <You kill me. I mean that. You think you can walk in here after all these years and pay wholesale? No way. Thats not

how this is going to play. You pay double. You pay double for what you did.>

Robbie says <What I did? Come on, Ketchum, I didnt do anything to you!>

Just like that the mood in the crib gets nasty. Neon lights go from pink to orange. Mass Effect switches to sleep mode. Ferret in the scarf starts choking on pistachio shells. Even Lil Wayne starts moaning ominous. Cuz Kyle is Kyle Ketchum, #69 Kyle Ketchum, the same infamous ass psycho that beat Robbie close to death with a beer pitcher back in the day. Lots a bewildering business starts making sense to my brain. How come Robbie didnt want to call the new dealer man. How come he put it off so long. These fat boys here were teammates long before sharkweek went south.

Ketchum says <You are one blind asshole. You cant see right in front of you.>

Robbie goes <Everyone liked Coach S. I know and Im sorry.>

Ketchum says <Who cares about everyone? Im talking about me.>

Robbie goes <Come on. We are adults now. Lets be mature.>

Ketchum says <Let me remind you about me. I screwed off in school. I dont think I finished a single test. But Coach S? Coach S was a stand up guy. Coach S was going to fix it up

for me. He was going to make some calls, get me a football scholarship, set me up for life, cuz he recognized I had talent out there blocking for your insane ass. Jesus, Robbie. You ever visit him in the hospital after what you did? You know how many operations he had to have? You know how painful it was? He ended up losing his family and everything cuz he wasnt the same man anymore. They shouldve forced you to visit, forced you to see what you did.>

Robbie goes <I understand. I do. But that was ten years ago.>

Ketchum says <Coach S didnt make phone calls for anyone after that. I had to make things work for myself. Well, here I am, and I got a bunch of boys under me. You think that was easy? You dont know. You dont deserve to know. All you got to know is this wasnt the plan. This wasnt the plan for me and it wasnt the plan for a whole bunch of guys depending on Coach S. And thats on you. All that is on you. To hell with double, you fat asshole. You want any of my stuff? Itll cost you triple. My opinion is you shouldnt even be allowed to use. You need to deal with what you did with a clear mind. Go see if anyone else will even talk to your Benedict Arnold ass.>

For a tired ass Mass Effect genius that used to be a blocker Ketchum has excellent speech skills. He picks up his ferret and kisses it all over its belly like we arent even there. Robbies face goes red as hell and its got nothing to do with how the neon changed colors again. Now blubber butt cant afford but a little sliver of the drugs he came for and thats doing a number on his self esteem.

Whole scenes got me feeling mixed up. Robbie said Im not his friend. Whats that about? But at the same time, Im feeling fat boy. Im feeling him hard. Theres no more Mrs Fullertons out there keeping tabs on his ass, you know? If hes got business to take care of, hes got to take care of it himself, just like #69 Kyle Ketchum did after Coach S got mangled. This whole town does Robbie same as Ketchum, unfair as hell, and tonight, with or without Ketchums drugs, theyre gonna be sorry.

Queen

Longside the razor blade candies and all them useless apples our drug haul amounts to just a pinch. All Robbie scored was a baggie a blow, a strip a acid, and a few pills a dust. Im glad Midge made herself scarce cuz our supermilk dreams are fading fast. Robbie pitches his nice black jacket to the floor and the Barenaked Ladies are soaked to his titties. Tits, tits, my bad. Robbie crosses his hairless tattoo arms across his soaked tits and takes in the whole pitiful spread. I cant even look. First the candies were chose poor. Then there werent enough blades. Now we dont have enough drugs? The plans doomed to fail just like all Robbies plans fail.

But hold up. Robbie doesnt bust any dishes. Doesnt chuck any stools. Doesnt smack himself on the head either. You can see inspiring spirit fill up his eyes. Business didnt go like he hoped with #69 Kyle Ketchum but what does Robbie care, you know? Its just one more betrayer in a life full a betrayers like his coach and his folks and his lawyer and Little Lamb. Robbies inspiring eyes tell me hes gonna use that stack of betrayers like firewood to power his ass forward like Boromir son of Denethor Steward of Gondor wanted real bad to use the One Ring against Mordor. Boromir was wrong but I think Robbies right.

Its coming up on three oclock and fat boy knows time is tight. He puts his fists on his hips and starts nodding and before he says a word Im proud a the chubby fool. Lets be real. This is it, yo. Robbies clocking out after tonight. This is his masterpiece and when its over the uniforms are gonna show up and drag Robbies ass to the joint. But the point is hes not gonna back down, hes not gonna step off, hes gonna run this play like he used to run the football, and hes gonna make the end zone one more time, you best believe.

He starts delivering orders and this time? Robocop, Im honored to be one of his Mission Impossibles. Im gonna prove to Robbie how Im a friend worth claiming next time someone asks. Robbie says, screw it. We worked hard and we did up some candies pretty good. But you know whatll do them up better than blades or blow? Chemicals. My brain starts imagining mad scientist stuff till Robbie opens a cabinet and takes out a big jug a Draino. Fat boys being all wise and teachery like Jesus. If you just open your eyes, he says, everything you need is right in front of you.

Robbie pulls out what paper hes got left from Ketchum. Just a sorry ass pile a singles. He jogs his lard ass to his bedroom closet and brings down this torched coffee pot where he keeps his secret bank. Sure isnt secret to me. I detectived that stash when I was just a wee little punk. But Im respectful of secret coffee pots and havent borrowed but fifty or sixty bucks over the years. No reason for Robbie to hide it anymore. In football they call this the two minute warning. He pours the whole pot a cash on top a the sexy witch and adds in the Ketchum singles and then he counts that mess out three times cuz Robbie doesnt have any more room for mistakes.

He takes fifty for himself and the rest he folds into my hand. Thats a nice suprise, right? He squats down next to me and shouts for Midget to get her ass in here and then he starts instructing me quiet and dramatic how I have one final job to Mission Impossible, how I got to run to Walgreen one final time. He yells for Midge again. He tells me trick or treats not but three hours away and we need some organization pronto in this bitch. My mission, if I choose to accept it, is to purchase the most poison ass products Walgreen sells and hustle my white ass back to Yellow Street.

So heres the rest of the plan. While I do a shopping spree, Robbies gonna turn the crib out and see what old chemicals hes got hiding. Divide and conquer, he says. Divide and mightyducking conquer! I dont interrupt his flow cuz hes going smooth but in my head I hope he does the bathroom closet first cuz thats pretty much the Robbie Museum of Natural History. Theres Robbie artifacts in there like you wouldnt believe. Whole set a silver ass silverware that must be a heirloom and a box full a satan books he stole from the library back when he tried to be a satanist. The whole story of his broken ass family is there if you know where to look.

Nuttiest thing I ever found inside was a box filled with dog junk. You know, junk for a dog. Heartworm treats and doggie shampoo and flea goop. Probably not toxic enough for putting on candies but dang. Who knew Robbie owned a dog? Its as mysterious as Lottes goldfish Ive never seen. Guess Robbie treated his dog good too. See, thats the kind a thing that makes you reevaluate a fat boy. Anyway further back theres also a bunch a crusty ass rusted ass corroded ass bottles a cleaning junk his folks musta bought before they scooted.

Robbie hollers for Midge again but all of a sudden shes right there. That kind a stealth ass behavior doesnt bother us much. Midgets always been a sneaky bitch. Except this time me and Robbie are spooked. Midgets shiny. Midgets straight up glistening. For a sec I think shes done herself up in jewels but that isnt it. Its flies. Girls covered in a thousand flies. I cant move. Cant say nothing. Robbie cant move or say nothing either. The smart part of my brain tells me to run away from that buggy mess fast as my short ass legs can go but the crazy part wants to wipe all them bugs away, cuz Midge is my sister, man, shes my sister.

Im freaking. Its like I dont want to see. Like I dont want to see nothing no more, not ever. Like I want to rip my eyeballs out so they have to give me a seeing eye dog with a special official vest and I can just pet it and never have to see nothing confusing or scary ever again. Focus, Jody. Look, little killer. You recognize that gunk. That sticky yellow gunk.

Flypapers, man. Midge wrapped herself in flypapers. Thats all it is. Three strips was all she got from the bachelor den but shes a tiny thing and she did herself up like the mummies we learned about that live under the sphinx. Little sisters wrapped so tight theres black bug guts smeared all over her arms and neck and face and that grody sight about makes me gag.

Worst part is how Midge is smiling. Shes happy as hell. These right here are her friends. Her best friends. Better than me, better than Dag. These are the friends she talks to special. Just look at her lips, shes whispering like theyre all her little serfs and shes their queen, a queen from a land like Middle Earth where a queen dresses up in the hides of her people, their dead bodies fueling her ass with their spirit and strength and whatnot, all a them extra legs and extra wings and extra eyes working overtime so nobody can get the drop on her. Whod be able to abuse a little ass girl when shes mighty queening like that? Right? Aint that right? Dang, man, just tell me thats right.

Fam

Situation in the crib is silent. Robbies covering his mouth tight. No mice are scurrying nowhere. Flypapers crackle like fire each time Midget breathes. I can feel it come. The itch. Its awful. Burns like I scratched myself everywhere. Heavy too like its scabbing over. The weight of all them scabs building and building like pressure. Pressing down hard. Like its gonna flatten our asses. Its us thats the flies, yo. You ever think a that? Like maybe the flies are us and all a us are gonna get swatted?

Robbie hasnt lived a life a courage but in these last hours things are changing. He reaches out. Cant believe my eyes. He reaches out, cups the side a Midges head, right by the ear, touching the sticky flypaper like he doesnt mind. His other hand comes out too. Im not prepared, not for this. His other hand comes out and cups my cheek the same way. Nothings ever been like this. I take hold a Robbies wrist with my left hand and hold the other side of Midgets neck with my right hand. I do it instinctive. Then the three a us are connected like fam and its powerful. Way up in my chest it stirs powerful as hell. I never felt nothing like it and the itch is gone and Im cool as the wind that blew the leaves in earlier, and I dont want none a it to end but of course its got to.

Robbie pets my hair with his thumb, faggot stuff, and I dont even care. He does the same to Midge and shes telling her flies all about it. Robbies all snotty and emotional and says I better be on my way. He shows us his last fifty bucks and says while Im at Walgreen hes gonna journey to McDonald and purchase us a feast. Use every last cent hes got cuz why not? We should have a huge ass last supper with all the tasty junk we enjoy best. Big macs, filet o fishes, nuggets, large pops, all that delicious stuff. He promises we will eat like we havent ever ate. We will celebrate fam. We will do it up right so we dont ever forget.

To My Little Lamb,

I didn't want to write this letter which is only the 3rd letter I've written by hand in my life but your Disrespectful & Hurtful actions forced me to or else I don't think I'd ever sleep again bc of how I'm sick all the time bc I wasn't treated like a Man. I'm sorry you have to read a Letter that'll hurt you also but if you knew how I can't eat & spend all night on a toilet you'd realize you're getting off Easy.

We used to be so loving to each other Little Lamb what happened? I remember like it was Yesterday you combing my hair with your sparkly fingernails & sure you were High & Drunk but you said I didn't deserve how everyone hates me & you never had a Man touch you so gently & although I was a Very Bad kisser & So Bad at sex I couldn't do it without Problems you didn't mind bc a Man can get better at those things but no Man can get better at gentleness.

I shouldn't have cried when you said that bc you probably lost Respect for me but Little Lamb you don't know what it felt like to be praised by someone & if that someone was a Beautiful Sexy Woman how it would make me feel like I was Worth Something for the first time in Many Years.

Now I just think you're a b****! You liked me well enough when I was bringing in Cold Hard Cash from my sign holding job. Back then you were like oh Robbie let's buy rum & cokes & weed & you used the word "we" but let's be honest about who was using his Cold Hard Cash to buy the things "we" wanted. I didn't care bc I loved you Little Lamb & maybe I shouldn't have told you I love you on the first night we were together especially right after I had sex Problems but I couldn't help it you were so Beautiful & Sexy & most of all Caring.

Do you even know why I lost my job holding signs you b****? It was bc the Turmoil I suffered when I found you f****** that guy Edgar which I suppose was forgivable since we'd only known each other a short time but still hurt bc you were doing it in my personal bed. You might think it's easy holding signs but I was crying so much I had to take my gloves off to wipe my tears unless I wanted oil on my face & then my hands got cold & I dropped the sign & when the foreman yelled at me I admit I swung my sign at him. Little Lamb you know Jody & Midget & Dag are at my house all the time & are Very Young & I can't have them seeing people f*** in my house even if it was me & you which it definitely Was Not.

I know you don't approve of Jody & Midget & Dag bc you have said it repeatedly & even said I was a Dirty Pedo which was cruel even if it was a joke. Those three kids are like family & I'm teaching them manners such as not using swear words as you can see in this Letter. Personally I think it's Adult people who are betrayers & Young people who accept you for the Friend you are. Little Lamb I hate to say this but your b**** ways have proven this to be true.

You know I forgave you for Edgar but I don't understand

why you had to f*** that banger Derek two days later once again in my personal bed. To be honest Little Lamb it made me wonder if you were a hooker! That was Very Hurtful & when I started crying & you laughed & said I should beat Derek's naked ass that was even More Hurtful bc it made me feel like I wasn't a Man. Derek also shouldn't have started salsa dancing on top of the bed with his d*** flopping around & shouldn't have gone into the kitchen Totally Naked to eat my food but this Letter isn't about that banger Derek it's about You & Me.

My life has been So Difficult Little Lamb! Every time you complained about the bulldozer noise it reminded me how I've lost everything & pretty soon will probably lose the house. You said you've had Hard Times too. So why couldn't our Hard Times bring us closer together? Instead you acted like it was a contest. I'd be like "They shut my water off" & you'd be like "Oh yeah well I have a UTI so shut up" & Little Lamb I've never had a girlfriend before but that's not how they act in movies!

I know you said you're not my Girlfriend & although I disagreed bc of the Highly Personal things I shared, maybe you were right bc why else would you f*** Butch in the backyard while I was making eggs & the very next day f*** Renny in the front yard while I was busy with diarrhea cramps? Imagine how ashamed you'd feel if Jody & Midget & Dag had come over that particular night. I bet you'd be Very Ashamed.

That is why I'm writing this Letter to Officially break up with you. I know you're going to say Robbie I've Only Known You For About Six Weeks & I Told You A Hundred Times I'm Not Your Girlfriend but I know you only said that to keep your heart from being broken which I understand better than anyone. My heart's broken so bad sometimes I cry all day which I know you hate & other times feel like I have no heart at all & also no lungs & no stomach & no spleen & I'm like the empty junk all over the lawn & after a while the emptiness fills up with Rage except at all the wrong times. For example not when you order me to beat up Derek but weird times like when I'm putting on a hemorrhoid pad or looking at a pretty sunset.

Little Lamb please don't try to win me back with your wiles. Don't come over looking Beautiful & Sexy & saying Caring things. I have had enough. I know you think Jody & Midget & Dag are using me but the one using me was you Little Lamb.

Since as I said this is only the 3rd letter I ever hand wrote my hand is cramping up like the tarantulas I bought last week to get over you & ended up having to murder. But I want to say one more thing. After I first met Jody playing in my front yard his mom invited me to his birthday party & I was Proud to go. I sold some junk to pay my water bill so I could shower before I attended & even though the party was all little kids in birthday hats which I'm sure makes you say I'm a Dirty Pedo, it made me So Happy. There were white kids & black kids & Asian kids & Middle East kids & Jody's mom said she was especially glad I was Jody's friend & I had to eat my birthday cake by the dumpster so no one could see my Tears of Joy.

Jody's mom is sick now with Jody won't say what, but I'll tell you Here & Now she's twice the woman you are Little Lamb. The second she saw me even though I've gotten fatter she knew who I was & the Violence in my past & still gave me a big hug & didn't call me a Life Ruiner like you did. That doesn't mean I don't know how I ruined Coach S's life. Trust me I know it!!! But you saw my Scrapbook & although you laughed so hard you sprayed eggs on it you saw the whole truth. Yes a Life Ruiner is one of the things I am, but does it have to be the Only Thing? I'm asking you does it? I know you don't like football but did you ever see the Very Famous Monday Night Football video of Joe Theismann's broken leg or the videos of Dennis Byrd or EJ Henderson or Marc Mariani? Back when I had internet I watched those videos All The Time to see athletes at The Top Of Their Game lose Everything from Catastrophic Injury. Maybe it sounds morbid but it made me feel like I wasn't Alone, like I just had my Catastrophic Injury a little earlier than they did.

Who knows maybe you're right about everything Little Lamb. Maybe Me & Jody & Midget & Dag don't deserve your Respect. But if that's true it's not bc we were born evil. Its bc we spent too much time on Yellow Street where Poison is everywhere & the immunity you build up fades away eventually & it's like my concussions where you can't see right anymore & can't hear right anymore & Do Not Know What You're Doing Anymore & the Poison leaks back out of you like sweat or piss or what didn't come out of me when we had our Terrible Sex.

If I'm a Life Ruiner Little Lamb it's my own life I'm ruining & no one can stop me.

Stay away forever,
Robbie

Dragon

Might snow after all. Trip to Walgreens cold as hell. Jean jacket isnt cutting it. I take me a sec to zip my zipper high and I peep three children done up like space dudes jumping over a gutter and piling themself in a car with two duck tape windows. I know exactly what those space dudes are up to. Back when Moms was mobile we did the same thing. Yellow Street candies suck balls. You want candies that dont suck balls, you get your ass drove to a hood thats got tall gates and good lawns. The ladies there do trick or treat like theyre in a contest. I used to get sparkle pouches full a incredible loot like candies with french on it or gold foil or salt which I know sounds foul but, robocop, hear me out, cuz salt on candies is sick.

Plenty a Yellow Street kids dont have wheels though so I expect words gonna travel fast Robbies passing out high quality treats. Thats what Im pondering when I spot Deformo a couple blocks away shuffling his deformed ass in my direction, probably after food but more likely to supply my punk brain gruesome nightmares forever. So I swerve hard on Dawson Ave and thats when boom I see Dag.

I stop sudden. Dags supposed to be home learning lesbian music with Piano Lady. But there she is, chilling in front of the grocery with the upside down carts and busted ass lottery signs. She hasnt changed clothes or nothing. Still wearing the red jacket with the zippers, still got scabs on her knuckles where she boxed Robbies light switch.

Dag was in a mood last time I saw her so I oughta walk by quiet. But its Dag! I wave my arms like a fool and just about yell <How you living, my ho?> but then I remember this is where we spied Gwendolyn this morning. Is Dag chasing that dog by herself? Whats up with that secretive sharkweek? She hasnt done that before. Or, dang, maybe she has. Maybe she does it regular. Maybe I dont know Dag so good after all. Theres a Christmas tree ornament on the cement thats still got a gummy price tag and I crunch it with my snowboot. Christmas? Nope. Christmas is never coming. Its gonna be Halloween forever.

For real, I got a mind to Walgreen my ass out a there. But I step closer just to get a better peep. Dags reaching out with what looks like a Dorito and her lips are saying soft sensitive junk to Gwendolyn whos just out a reach shivering real low like dogs do. A little closer, I see how Dags trailed a whole Dorito trail to lure the dog but that dog aint falling for it. Cant tell for sure but Dag might be crying cuz a her huge emotions. Now theres no way I can run off to Walgreen. How am I supposed to leave my best bitch?

A big brave feeling grabs me. Dags fixed on Gwendolyn, right? And Gwendolyns fixed on Dag? Neither a thems paying attention to me. So I get my creep on and sneak my short ass behind this car without any wheels or doors. I get on my stomach navy seal style and crawl behind this cardboard hill that looks like Deformo probably squats there and I do it easy cuz you know how tight my abs are. Now Im close enough to hear their asses, how Dags all desperate and sad and Gwendolyns moaning and crunching her Doritos both.

The layouts ideal. Longside the grocery front theres stacked a rusty old washing machine and a big blue postal box on its side and I get right up behind it with Gwendolyn three feet away tops. I pause to get some breaths in and wish I had some a Robbies dog stuff. Doggie toys or doggie rawhide treats, any a that stuff would help right now. Robbie might even know special tricks about how to get a dog to let you be nice. Robbies not here though. I got to do this by myself. I peek around the washing machine real slow and the dogs right there. Right now is when I need to steady hero this scene.

I leap like a jaguar! Gwendolyn flattens her filthy ass to the cement and Dag cusses a cuss word and then boom, I hit the ground with my arms and legs caging that wild animal. She goes crazy like shes one big hairy muscle, clenching and twisting, but I bust out my courage and stick my hands in that hairy mess and even though theres hot breath and sharp claws flying all over, I grip a hand around a skinny leg and a arm around some bony ass ribs and next thing you know I rock back to my knees and I got that mutt! I got that scraggly ass, mud covered, broke tail having mutt!

Dags shocked. Real shocked. I try to give her a smile but its hard with this street beast wiggling and chomping. I squeeze tight till some a her fight goes away and then I stand up and hold that dog proud. Dag looks like shes about to poop. I start laughing and I come up to Dag cuz this is what shes been waiting for forever. Not winning class vice president or best debator or top piano bitch. Dags truest wish is to pet this filthy animal and her man made it happen. Her man. Thats me. Hey maybe Dag and me can take care of her together. Maybe Gwendolyn can be my seeing eye dog with a official vest if I do end up scooping my eyeballs out one day.

Last thing I need is this animal taking a piece out a Dag though so I dig my fingers deep in its tangled up fur. Hold up, hold up. Things dont feel right. I stop walking and feel closer with my fingers. Gwendolyns skin isnt normal. Feels knobby and squooshy like bubble wrap. I hitch the dog up in one arm and brush the fur back so I can get a look. Wheres her skin at? I cant find any pink skin. Wait up. Aw, hell no. Hell no. No, no, no.

Ticks! Hundreds a ticks! Hiding right under the fur! Big ticks, small ticks, black ticks, brown ticks, yellow ticks, green ticks, red ticks, orange ticks, so many theyre piled like grapes. The dogs shining in the sun cuz a all them fat glossy ticks. I get a disgusting shiver down my back cuz Im touching all a them plump ass blood filled suckers, and when I move my hand even a little the fattest ones pop and bleed out hot. Sharkweek! Sharkweek! I dont even know what to do! Im just standing there holding that sick oozy bitch!

Dags covering her face with both hands. Dorito dusts smearing all over her cheeks. She starts whining too, at least thats what I think first. But that aint Dag. Thats the dog. I look down and Gwendolyn looks up and even though Ive seen her a billion times its like I never saw her for real. Eyes crapped up with brown scum worse than pinkeye. Nose crusted shut. Gums super puffy and red. And shes shaking. Shaking rough.

The dogs done fighting her doggie fight. I can tell. Shes not even a dog no more. Shes a ball a ticks sucking her ass dry till shes just a bag a fur. Just like the whole town is sucking Robbie dry, just like I said. Gwendolyn looks at me the way I bet she looked at the evil maniac that abandoned her ass on the street. Its the look of trust. Dogs trusting me to do what needs done.

I set Gwendolyn on the cement and she tucks her legs up under. Me and Dag squat close. Shes not gonna bite. She aint got any bite left in her. When Dag holds a Dorito in front a Gwendolyns mouth, she sticks out a pale ass tongue and licks it but its like shes just doing Dag a favor. Me and Dag havent said a single word. Both a us are petting that dog right over the ticks. Its ill as hell but dang. Theres nothing else to do.

My stainless steel throwing disc is the finest weapon I ever owned. Its not even a contest. Whenever I slide it out of its free of charge nylon pouch I feel full a the magic and mystery of the orient. Its not about ninjas dropping ninjas. Its about being a monk, being for peace and accepting your fate, plus also the fate of everything great and small. Case you forgot, my throwing disc is shaped like a circle but its split into three scythes like a grim reaper has and each a them joins up in the middle in a impressive dragon shape.

I pull aside some a the fur on Gwendolyns throat and scrape off a few ticks and puts a scythe right against her neck. When the dog whimpers it vibrates the stainless steel dragon and its like the dragons whimpering too. Dag scooches over and holds my shoulder. Her face is closer to mine than its ever been before and she isnt worried about catching my pinkeye or nothing.

Gwendolyns broke ass tail starts wagging. Wagging cuz she knows. Sharkweek. Sharkweek. Robbie treated his old dog good, right? Far as I can tell he did. Right here I need to try and do just as good, do what a mans supposed to do. Except I dont want to be a man no more, all right? Im just gonna be a little ass kid, okay? Im gonna climb into some nice ass car and trick or treat my ass over in the fancy hood where all the dogs are alive and happy. All right?

Dags crying dry. More like coughing. Like shes run out a liquid. Those are the miserable facts too. Yeah, Dag has her a moms and a pops and a piano lesbian and teachers and math friends and fellow fluters, all that stuff. The truth, though? Shes aloner than me. The only companion she had for real was Lotte and Lotte doesnt exist anymore. Lottes just a address where Dag mails beautiful paper. I mean, look. Dags not stopping the dragon. Dags not saying <No, Jody, dont do it.> She could try all day to save her sister or save this dying ass dog. But whats the right thing to really do? You know good as me and I guess Dag knows it too. Shes got to cut both them bitches loose and its my duty to man up, be the monk, help out the best I can.

Walgreen 2

We hit the door, door does its ding ding, and first thing I do is make tracks to the Halloween aisle and dig up Barack Obama. The eye holes are small and help me only see the stuff that needs being seen. When youre Barack Obama theres no looking back. No looking sideways either. You look straight ahead like a pimp twenty four seven and thats how I plan to roll from here on out.

Once Im incognito I scope out the register. Dick Trickle must a got his child abusing ass canned cuz beer belly goatee manager mans the one scanning products. Thats a relief cuz its four in the afternoon and greedy ass children are gonna start knocking on doors any second. Now where did Dag run off? I explained the score on the way over and even though she didnt say much she stood tall like a trooper and pulled the chip right outta my pocket. Shes real eager to get a head start shopping.

Monster Mash keeps blasting outta the speakers. Thats a dope joint, no doubt, but the third time through Im about to tear my ears off. Finally I peek my mask around the fancy soap corner and theres Dag. Shes got a plastic Walgreen basket heaped with boxes and bottles and shes scowling at a label hard cuz shes what teachers call a good critical reader. Girlfriend looks fierce when shes serious. Man, I never knew a honey so fierce and smart. Theres fancy ass hand towels hanging there and I try to wipe my hands clean. Dags acting strange since we did Gwendolyn and I dont think she needs to see all that blood.

Barack Obama dances out doing the Monster Mash cuz I figure its humorous but Dags critical reader face doesnt change. She lets me hold the basket like a mans supposed to but Ill be honest. Dags collected so much lethal ass junk it makes my stomach hurt. Shes got rust remover. Oven cleaner. Ant spray. Carpet shampoo. Superglue. Jewelry cleaner. Weed killer. Extremely flammable. Will cause fetal effects. Will inflame lungs. May cause dizziness. Can cause severe burns. Will produce poisonous gas. Flush eyes with cold water. Induce vomiting. Call poison control center immediately. So many hazards my throat clogs up like Im the trick or treater that just gobbled the whole basket.

I start trying to slow her ass down. Robocop, I dont even know why. But I get super distractionary. Im like <Yo, Dag, wait up, how about this coconut foot creme?> and she shakes her head but I keep on like <Yeah, I know its not that dangerous but smell it, it smells delicious and no kiddies are gonna eat candies that smell like weed killer, you know?> and she takes the tube right outta my hand and chucks it on the floor. I got to fake like Im not shocked and so Im like <Youre right, coconuts gross, its like eating pubes, right?> Dag doesnt even answer.

Bitch shops so hard I cant keep pace. She doesnt even browse her favorite section even though we finally have the funds to buy the most beautiful Lotte papers ever made. Instead what she does is basket up some personal items for Robbie, deodorant and mouthwash and whatnot, and I think its real thoughtful before I realize theres nothing thoughtful about it. Robbies got to look normal and smell normal or arent any parentals gonna let their juniors accept his treats. Dag understands that stuff cuz Dags a girl. But it itches me. Its cold, man. And colds just not how Dag usually is. Usually Dags emotions zoom all over the room.

Dag makes for the register and I think about all the other stuff we could buy with Robbies cash. We could buy us a burner phone. We could phone us a uniform, spill the truth totally anonymous so Robbie wouldnt know who told. We could buy a scooter that fits both a us and scooter our asses away fast as hell, forever and ever. Or we could buy bandages and antiseptic and spend Halloween with Moms fixing up her sores and saving her from Judge Mathis and Mario Lopez and not thinking about whats going down on Yellow Street. If you got the cash theres nothing you cant do, nobody you cant help.

By the time I catch up to Dag, goatee managers scanning and Dags flashing the green and goatee managers saying our chips short twenty five bucks. I feel relief! Then it takes one second to start feeling bad about feeling relief. This is Dag here. This is Robbie. Dag and Robbies my closest people. No ones ever supported my ass like they do. So when Dag does skillful subtraction and removes a few items I dont say jack. Beer belly goatee manager man scans again and it totals the exact number of dollars we have. That oughta be what Im feeling relief about. Maybe if I try harder I can feel it.

Goatee manager man points to my face and asks if we want to buy that too. Say what? Am I gonna buy my own dang self? Its like Im in some kind a supermilk fantasy. Does this mean Jody himself is a poison chemical product? Does this mean we can decide to purchase my ass or not and the choice is up to us? Cuz if thats the case then thats the biggest relief of all cuz that decision is easy. What we need to do is put me back on the shelf before I cause anybody more harm.

Course what he refers to is Barack Obama. I peel him off and theres nowhere presidential to put him so I set him real gentle on the floor. Dang. Look at that. Hes all inside out and pink and wet. He looks like roadkill. It gives me a sad feeling. All that powerful Barack Obama power I had is flattened out. Dag pays up and Im just standing there staring. Like a zombie. Whispering Monster Mash to a roadkill president. I dont even do it on purpose. Song bubbles out a me natural. How its a graveyard smash. How it catches on in a flash. All that stupid, stupid sharkweek.

Dag hands me both bags outside. Not in shortys whole life did she ever act this hard. She informs me shes got to go eat dinner with her folks. I ask her how come and she says shes got a big test on Watership Dog on Monday and her folks are gonna quiz her ass at dinner and thats nonnegotiable. I shrug like it aint no thing but she steps to like I burned her. Its weird, yo. She says she emphasized to her folks shes got trick or treat responsibilities tonight so its gonna be a early dinner and shes gonna be back to Yellow Street quick as crap. Girlfriend says it like a threat. Like shes suspecting Im plotting to ditch these bags and screw up Robbies whole thing.

Just to cool her ass out I asks if Watership Dog is about pirate dogs cuz pirates, plus also dogs, are the funnest stuff they let you learn at school. Dag stares me down like a gangsta. She says its called Watership Down, not Dog, and its not about pirates, or dogs either, its about rabbits. I go like <Oh> and shes like, yeah, its about a warren a dumb rabbits with faggot names and the lesson is how you got to run away if you want to survive. I go like <Oh> but now shes snarling how the only rabbit she respects is this dude Woundwort that surrounds his easter bunny ass with soldiers that bite off the ears a traitors. I go like <All right> and Dag just stares. Dags real good at staring all of a sudden.

After that creepy information she takes off but I holler her back cuz I forgot to tell her about the McDonald feast Robbie promised and if she eats too much Pinebluff Glenn Estates food shes gonna miss out. Dag looks doubtful cuz Robbie promised supermilk earlier and that sure as hell didnt happen. But her doubtful face makes her look more like good old Dag so I swear to her how this time fat boys coming through. Truth is I dont have a clue if thats the case. But Dag at least looks hopeful. Like she still believes in me a little. Thats all it takes for me to get sprung! Yeah, girl. Thats right. Jodys got your back for eternity.

This time she leaves for real and I stand there being chilly and hoping my shorty remembers to wear her special secret Halloween costume. Lots a junk going down tonight and itd suck balls if she forgot. Now that Midget mummied her ass up in flystrips I oughta focus on my own disguise. Walgreens right here and for a sec I consider slinking my ass back inside to see if I can snowboot more Grishnákh junk. Some Grishnákh junk at least if not the whole dang mightyducking Barack Obama.

Dick Trickle 2

<I sweat to you I will not let the white city fall, nor our people fail.>

Believe, yo. Im getting exhausted with ignorant ass fools misreading my jean jacket like I markered it up for their private personal jokes.

<I sweat to you? What kind of drivel is that?>

Homeboys love to read it out loud sarcastic cuz in this part of town theres like a rule how no ones allowed to care about anything, not even if its a masterpiece of motion picture cinema. All youre supposed to do out here is chase pussy and talk smack and acquire a black hoodie to wear on top a your XXXL whitey. But this voice isnt making fun. It sounds serious. Not Éomer son of Théodwyn serious but pretty serious. I square up before I turn around just in case I need to defend Peter Jackson and his Oscar winning trilogy more time.

<Swear. Oh. I swear to you. Still sounds like horse feathers.>

Dick Trickle? Like I need this right now? Bony maloney is sitting his skeleton ass on the curb. Never seen him out from the counter before and check it, his ancient ass has legs and feet and everything except one a his legs is gimpy and the shoes got a special heel. Dont worry, his disability doesnt get me feeling a crumb a sympathy. Hes still got the usual Dick Trickle face like he thinks I peed in his old person medicine.

Heres the thing. He isnt burning up a cig. I always figured him for a high commitment nicotine freak cuz he guarded the Walgreen smokes so dang hard. Instead his big old dentures are chomping a celery stick. Hes got a thermos too that looks like a smoothie but not a good smoothie with ice cream, one with fruit, which is gross, and vegetables, which is even grosser. Maybe its the Walgreen lights but Dick Trickle dont look so phantomy out here. Old as hell but healthy. He chomps his celery and nods his bald spot head at my jacket.

He goes <What is that, some kind a gang garbage?>

See? Here we go. Now I double wish Id thefted Barack Obama so this creaky ass civil rights mightyducker couldnt get in my grill. That bulls the last bull I got patience for today. I hike up the chemical bags and set to leaving but the dude is like <I asked you a question, young man> so I do a thug turn and roll up on that fogey like hes gonna get bruised.

He takes a drink of veggie smoothie like hes got all the time in the world. Dont he know what day it is? Hasnt he ever checked a clock? Things are about to go wild on Yellow Street and he chooses this exact time and place to mess with me? I drop my bags and swagger up and say <Im my own dang gang, gramps. You wanna scrap? Show me your play, old man, lets see it.>

The sun is direct in his face and I can see the lines dug deep in his skin like bark on a big old tree and its like this old dudes probably been taking breaks on this curb since before I was born and is gonna be taking breaks on this curb long after whatever happens to me tonight happens to me. Old timers still flashing his nametag so I guess goatee manager man didnt can his ass. Not that it matters none. Walgreen goes outta business, burns down, whatever, this dinosaurs gonna outlive all us fools, rabbiting all the worlds celery like hes from Watership Dog.

He goes <You talk like a Saturday cartoon. I cant understand a single word you say.>

<Cuz youre a deaf mightyducker!> Thats what I say.

He goes <Is that why you write things on your jacket? Because you have trouble speaking?>

Ooo! I punch my palm and do a circle walk so I dont bank his ass! Im like <How come you got a problem with me, old man? Every time Im over here youre bugging!>

He goes <Whats on your hands? Is that blood?>

And I go <Thats none a your business, senior citizen!>

And hes like <Gracious, son. You have blood on your hands.>

And Im like <Mightyducker, Im not your dang son!>

Then he goes <You literally have blood on your hands. Gracious me.>

So I go <Then sell me some wet wipes! Aisle four, bitch!>

Two black folks walk by on their way to Walgreen and they spot Dick Trickle and instead of avoiding him they smile and head right up. The man is a sharp looking brother, handsome as hell. If Dags dads George Clooney, this dudes Idris Elba. He gives Dick Trickle a dap and asks hows Dick Trickles living, and then Idris Elbas honey that looks like Rihanna leans over and plants her pretty red lips right on Dick Trickles withered ass cheek. How the dang hell do all these sexy black superstars know this crusty old brontosaurus? They go like <Well be seeing you Sunday> and Dick Trickle chuckles like <You know you will> and I just got to stand there alone steaming mad while Dick Trickle gulps a gulp of health drink before remembering Im standing there. He sighs big and rubs his bony hand across his face like hes trying to iron out sixty five million years a wrinkles.

<You asked what my problem is. Ill tell you. Young men like yourself, I see you every day. Here at the store. Over on Golden Boulevard where I attend service. Such a waste. Such a waste of youth and energy and spirit. The Bishop preaches that we the congregation are at fault. We let our children run too far and now they wont come back. Even hearing us older folk talk has become an affront to the young. I dont debate the Bishop on that. But on one point he and I disagree. Ultimate responsibility, young man, lies with you. Not with us.>

Old mans interrupted my flow. My comeback is weak.

<You gonna sell me those wet wipes or what?>

Dick Trickle takes a second celery stick from his plastic bag. Man, I wish he did smoke so I could bum a heater cuz its colding up by the second and my teeth are rattling. But this old skeleton? His crooked ass leg and those skinny ass arms? Not a single bone on him is shaking.

<Delinquency is nothing new, son. I wasnt any different in my time. Here is my advice on this October evening. Here is my advice to you, which of course you will ignore. You have to get yourself right with the Lord. Thats the only way to take yourself off this crooked path.>

I go like <What path? You think Im going to acquire me a nice shiny Walgreen nametag one day? Punch the clock for some pimply ass goatoe haver? Youre one dense ass robocop. Look at all the great stuff the Lord did for your worshipful ass. Busting poor ass children for taking extra candy? Security cameraing my boy Robbie so he cant buy what he needs to live right? Thats your life? Hell, no. The Lord hasnt done sharkweek for your shriveled up ass so why the hell would he do sharkweek for mine?>

He goes <You talk like some kind of cartoon. I literally cannot understand your words. Youve gone and invented a language nobody can speak and then you wonder why nobody speaks to you with respect. But I believe we are in agreement. I

got right with the Lord after a time but I know plenty of people who have not. I see them every day. Young fellows in wheelchairs. Old men with one lung or bad arteries or cancer of the tongue, smoking away their paychecks.>

Four dang thirty in the p.m. and the suns razor blading the bald center of this old farts fro. Dark rolled up rapid tonight. People are checking the sky all surprised when they come out the automatic door. How many times have I seen that door ghost open and ghost shut? Tonight goes like I think its gonna go and this could be the last time in history I see this Walgreen. Dang, man. That feels weird to think. Whos gonna bust the balls of Salvation Army Santa if Im not around? Whos gonna bust the balls of Dick Trickle?

When the door shuts and the Monster Mash is sealed in, no cars come by for a bit and the only thing I hear is leaves crabbing their monster claws across the cement. If thats the real life sound of the night then I better keep talking and talking and talking cuz what if that cold ass click clacking is all I can hear when Im stuck all alone inside some juvie cage like Robbie used to be?

I go <You keep your Lord, all right? You keep your gangs. I dont need them.>

Hes like <If that isnt gang garbage on your jacket then I apologize. Honestly those words might be the best thing you have going. Reminds me of something the Bishop might say. About saving the city, about how you cant let your people fail.>

Dick Trickle shrugs and his prehistorical face gets even darker cuz the suns stuck behind public housing. <It sounds heroic. Sounds like the words of a hero. Is that why you wear them on your back?>

For a sec it gets me thinking. What if the cobwebby old geezer is right? What if the whole reason I feel Lord of the Rings so powerful and wrote it on my jean jacket is so that the marker can soak through to my skin and I can start fighting for the forces of good. Those two superstars that dapped and kissed Dick Trickle, his church on Golden Boulevard, this Bishop dude he keeps mentioning. Its like Dick Trickle is the real deal. He dont need no Barack Obama mask. Hes got so much fam hes got to celery up to stay healthy so he dont die and all his loved ones cry forever. What do I got? All I got? I got this jacket trying to inject Peter Jacksons inspirations into my veins.

But I cant help it, I go <Never mind your stale minimum wage ass why I do any a the stuff I do! You got that, robocop? Say what? Cant understand your old man cartoon language either behind them filth ass dentures! You best report cuz Im about to punch you in the dang dick, you hear? You hear me, you geriatrical dicksuck punk?>

Thats what I say.

The truth though is Im wondering.

Feast

The McDonald feast is torn up. Cant believe my eyes. Its like somebody got terrorist bombed. Whole cribs splattered. Mangled ass hamburger stomped into the carpet like brain. Bits a nugget and chicken tender flung across the chair like muscle. Fries smushed into everything like white flesh. And ketchup. Ketchup like you cant believe, striped on the walls and goobering the clocks. Before I recognize the McDonald wrappers I figure Robbie decided to skip past all that candy nonsense, and this mess is whats left of some poor ass child that came knocking early.

First thing I think is oh no. Did my Midget survive this? Cuz I tell you what, lettuce and tomato and onion and pickle looks a lot like little girl guts. But sisters making a soft noise and there she is squatted in the same corner as before except now shes got a chunk a McRib. Shes chewing and whispering to her dead ass flypaper flies and this time theres no doubt shes saying the name DAndre. And thats not all. I hear Antoine and Shonelle and Cassandra and Michael and Jemarcus and Sharise and Eric and Jada too. Naw, man. Thats too many. Too many fly names. Cuz what if all their asses were messed up bad as DAndre? What if Midges been carrying around every single one a them inside her head?

The flies are multiplying like crazy. Theres maggots all over little sisters green sweaties. Im losing my mind, man. Im losing my mind. I swear Im gonna jump in, grab them squirmy worms in my fists, and squeeze till they goop out. I dont give a dang if Midget gave them maggots names or not, theres no space left in the world for traumatic little fly babies. Lucky for me Ive got a little bit of sense left cuz it turns out theyre not maggots. Theyre sesame seeds. Midge musta ate a bun.

Robbie staggers in. Fat boys a whole new level a fat. Maybe its just my furious mind. But the Barenaked Ladies are stretched so tight its like they have Downs. Robbies weaving like hes drunk. Face red as hell, belching wet, stumbling like hes gonna take a header. His whole outfit is plastered with McDonald. Mustard and barbecue and mayonnaise and special sauce. Its like he took a bath in that junk. My favorite shirts stained fatal and hes got cheddar cheese caught in his hairdo. Theres just no doubt. No doubt at all. Fat boy promised us a feast and then feasted it all himself. Like a punk. Like a pig. Like a piggy ass pig face punk.

Something snaps. Feels real as a couple years back when Robbie stomped and broke my toe. I start shaking serious and wheezing like Im one a them poor ass asthma kids in gym. Its not right. This behavior here is not right. This feast was for all a us. For me and Dag and Midget. We havent ate all day. Now its just grease. Just smears a grease on top a the grease already greased over everything. Whole cribs nothing but grease from stuff that once upon a time was clean.

Brother DAndre is who I feel like. Bunch a busted ass parts sealed up inside stupid cement and rotting away where nobody can see. If I break off that cement, a big chunk a me is gonna break off with it. But mightyduck it. You feel me? I dont care what breaks off. Im itchy under there so bad and cant take none a this no more.

McDonald guts feel good and warm. Get me two big handfuls before I start throwing. Robbies halfway through a burp when it hits, a big eyeful a honey mustard goop and cheddar jack slime from a chicken wrap. It splashes across his face and its not funny. It looks like hes been shot, like the mess bursted from his insides. Midget gasps and cuts out her buggy conversations but thats the last thing I care about cuz Im wild, Im a animal, Im grabbing McDonald slop off the floor and screaming how Robbies a fuck, a fat fucking shit ass fuck, and thats what I say, the genuine fucking f word and shit ass s word too, cuz I dont care about what a fucking childs supposed to fucking say, Robbies a motherfucking terrible fat adult shitfucker that shits all over his fucking motherfucking friends that fucking do all they fucking can to keep his motherfucking shit tight as fucking possible and the shit ass motherfucker doesnt appreciate it one fucking bit or treat little fuckers like little fuckers oughta be motherfucking treated. Shits splashing Robbie all over. Cheese melt. Tartar sauce. Hickory smoke bacon. Mushrooms. Some a it backsplats on me and it doesnt taste any better than the snot sliding down cuz Im sobbing like a little bitch. Fuck Robbie, you know? Fuck all grown ass adults. Miss Poole from school and Dick Trickle from Walgreen and Mrs F from the nice part of town and Moms and my lets be honest probably white as fuck pops too cuz none a them helpless adult fuckers are helping none a us kids far as I can see. Just look at this sorry shit. Little sisters nibbling a McRib with her fucking hands! Theres supposed to be a table, yo. A table for little motherfuckers to eat their food from. And forks and knives and shit. Napkins to wipe your fucking face like youre civilized after you clean your plate. And plates! Fuck, man! You got to have fucking plates to clean in the first motherfucking place! Naw, motherfucker! Aint none a this shit gonna stand! Midge is a baby, yo! A baby! She cant grow up in a filthy ass world that aint got any way out except ending up like Robbie or #69 Kyle Ketchum or one of them motherfucking Halloween children walking down the fucking block to their doom right this fucking second.

Robbie stands there and takes it. Hes got onion in his hair and a pickle glued to his cheek. It looks like hes crying chipotle. When I run out a McDonald I throw everything I can, a computer mouse and a hockey puck and a beautiful geode rock. The rock knocks Robbie right in the ear but he doesnt do anything except blink even after the blood comes. Under his flab he looks just like a scared little child. Like us, like no better than us, and if thats true how are we supposed to make it? It makes me crazy sad and that makes me even madder but I dont got anything left to throw, I cleared a bald patch in the living room and now Im slipping around a big orange puddle a McDonald juice.

Im on my ass now with my drawers soggy with sauce but I pull the Grishnákh stuff out a my snowboots, fake teeth and purple ass face paint that wasnt the right shade anyhow, and I throw that too and it makes me heartbroken as hell cuz I had plans, you know? I had plans a doing that stuff up right so Dag thought I was smart and creative and now shes never gonna know, nobodys ever gonna see all the things Ive got imagined inside my head.

Shower

Last thing left to throw is my ninja stars and I feel Gwendolyns crusty blood on the stainless steel. Up pops a video in my head of me doing Robbie the same way, how his fat jelly neck slices open and black evil blood shoots out. But heres the question killing me. Does dropping Robbie have the same mercy to it as dropping a tick sucked doggie? Hows anyone supposed to know for sure?

Whole cribs full a noises I cant stand. Midget whining cuz shes spooked. Robbies stomach squirting cuz a all the McDonald. And me doing hiccups cuz Im a boo hooing bitch. I drop my ninja tools, all of them, and kick every single one into floor trash and use a sleeve a my jacket, the one that says <THEY HAVE A CAVE TROLL> and who knows, yo, maybe the cave troll is me, and I take that sleeve and wipe all the hot emotional goo off my face. Emotional goo wont get none a us nowhere. Doesnt matter what Dick Trickle said about crooked paths. Midget, Dag, Robbie, me, this is the path we four are walking. We better accept it. This is the path and one a us has to step up, lead the way. Why not me? What else am I here for?

Walgreen bags are still sitting where I dropped them. I fish around inside and pull out the deodorant and mouthwash and cologne Dag got and I throw them at Robbies feet.

<Put your fat ass in the shower> I say and it comes out scary weak. I huck back some snot and do a do over. <No kid is gonna take candy from a stank ass freak.>

I dont look at Robbie when I say it. Dont look at anything. All I look at is the back a my eyelids but the problem with being a human person is you cant close your ears no matter how bad you want and clear as hell I hear Robbie lean over and fart and pick up the deodorant and mouthwash and cologne and shuffle his footsteps real slow across the room, thump thoomp, and through the McDonald trash, crinkle crunkle, and into the bathroom where the shower starts firing in spurts like it does, like a cut throat bleeding out, split splat sploot.

Music

House stinks like eggs cuz the waters bad on Yellow Street. Robbies outta the shower and shining like a whale cuz a the Total Body Hair Removal. His tats are on full display. Hes got a Jesus cross on his arm and a mean mongoose on his back and what looks like a push lawnmower high up on his leg though I guess that cant be right. None a them are inked with skill and all a them are uglied up with pimples.

I wish I could quit looking. Not cuz Robbies blubber butt revolts me but cuz hes sick. Fat boys sick as hell. First time he puked it went on so epic me and Midget went in there to get a look and both a us gots our minds blown. There was a whole mountain a McDonald in that toilet. Cant believe a mammal put that much food down in the first place. Robbies got a bad DT tremble and hes holding the towel rack so he dont fall. Hes pale as hell. Even his lips are pale. Me and Midge hurried our asses out a there but not before I peeped the shower. Looks like fast food soup. Lettuce and tomato and meat clogging the drain so bad the waters just floating there pink.

Second and third time Robbie puked we didnt go look.

Midgets the one that spots trick or treaters first. Little sister taps the window real hyper till I come see. Theres no mistaking it. Its a momma and two sons dressed like smurfs or blueberries or something else blue. Right now theyre strolling the other side a Yellow Street but theyll be circling to our turf soon enough. Its five thirty. Already late. Too late to be thinking about changing the plan. I pound me some yoga breaths like Miss Poole taught and clear my mind of all the junk up there cuz, look, when you lose your yoga mind? Thats when things go rough. I pick up the Walgreen bags. Simple. I go in the kitchen. Real simple. Be the monk.

Robbie lied so much today he deserves a olympic medal in lying. But he didnt lie about this. He said he was gonna turn out the crib for chemicals and thats exactly what fat boy did. He has it set out in neat rows on top a the sexy calendar witch. Theres a rusted ass can a WD40 that says <harmful or fatal if swallowed>. Bottle a Scotchgard he must a bought back when he had a car. Tube a paste called Kwik Seal Plus that says <this product contains chemicals known to the State of California to cause cancer>. Biggest jug of all is labeled Clorox Toilet Bowl Cleaner and even though it <causes irreversible eye damage> I chuck it under the counter to save it cuz Robbies toilet is gonna need big time disinfection later.

Also Lysol and Borax and Oxi Clean and D Con Rat Killer and Raid Max Concentrated Deep Reach Fogger. Do all adults collect poisonous stuff like a hobby? Once youre grown I guess you spend a lot a time thinking about junk in your life you oughta scrub away. But for a fat boy sitting on the can right now diarrheaing out his last meal its a impressive spread. He did his part. I got to give him that. Time I do mine.

Bowls. Whered they go? Dang. Theyre drowned in the foul ass sink. Being clean doesnt matter though so I set out each bowl on the table and fill each a them with chemical. It burns. Didnt expect so bad a burn. Eyes are burning and nostrils are burning and lungs are burning and the skin by my fingernails is burning too. The positive side is that the fumes clear my mind better than yoga breaths and now Im floating. Pouring and burning and floating and smiling too even though my teeth ache cold.

Midget helps unwrap candies cuz thats the sort a stuff is super enjoyable for a young ass child. Then we dip. Dip in, dip out. Doesnt take much thinking. Real simple. Our skin is irritating though so I fetch spoons from the sink to dip more safe. Just like doing easter eggs is what I tell Midge and that makes it funner. I instruct little sister how to do it perfect and she catches on good. She doesnt even fuss much when one a her flypaper flies falls in a chemical and croaks. I fetch us a fork too cuz it helps make holes in the candies so the chemicals soak better. We work it fast. Fast and simple.

Robbie comes in and has a brown towel around his fat belly and shaving cream on his fat face. He doesnt look our way. He takes a bottle a Mad Dog hes got hid above the fridge and takes a big old pull before he leaves. Hes not acting normal so I sneak a bathroom peek. Fat boys shaving close. Blood running wild and dots of toilet paper stuck all across his cheeks. Second time I peek hes got underwear on the bottom and on top a shirt Ive never seen thats got buttons and a collar. Third time I peek he has a tie and hes trying to tie it. Thats when the itch comes right back outta the fumes. A tie? I never expected to see Robbie in a tie till he was in a coffin.

Midget finishes chemicalling candies by herself cuz watching Robbie style himself has captivated my ass while the itch keeps growing. Robbies no good at elegant stuff. His tie knots a big loose fatty. Colognes spilled all across the counter grime. Belts too small cuz a his unbelievable fat. Whole time hes wheezing like hes nervous as hell so about once a minute he does a shot a Mad Dog and follows it up with a shot a mouthwash to hide it.

Puking and pooping uncontrollable isnt a good way for a man to go out. Robbie needs to zen out if events are gonna go better than they went with #69 Kyle Ketchum. So I hatch a idea and visit the garage bachelors den and bring inside the boombox and the Illustrated World Encyclopedia of Guns and fat boys all time favorite number one CD. I put the Illustrated World Encyclopedia of Guns on top a the CD lid but when I press play it just skips and skips and I get a ill stomach same as Robbie.

Guess who saves the day? Midget. She removes the Illustrated World Encyclopedia of Guns and picks up the CD with her chemical burn fingers and squints her red fume eyes at a bunch a brown spots on the bottom I think are Natural Light. Little sister yanks out a poof a her green sweaties between the flypapers like shes yanking out intestines and she uses the poof to wipe the CD real fastidious. Sister gives it back and this time when I press play it plays.

Must a heard this CD a million times back in the day. Hated it a million times too. I dont know, man, Barenaked Ladies just isnt my jam. But I play that junk to soothe out Robbie and Im straight up stunned how good it works. Robbie hears it and grips the bathroom sink and gives his styled ass a long hard look in the mirror and sighs out a big steady sigh. I bet hes thinking what Ive been thinking. Dont think too much. Do things simple. He closes the toilet cuz he wont be needing a toilet anymore.

He plops his fat ass on the lid and dresses himself in nice pants and nice socks and regular ass shoes and then sets to buttoning his buttons which he has a hard time with. I watch Robbie how I expect a child watches his pops when his pops is prepping for work. Something happens. Im not sure when exactly. But at some point I start feeling feelings. Robbie, his nice ass clothes, the Barenaked Ladies. Them fools are singing about growing up and how its scary and challenging and whatnot. But its like theyre singing about Robbie who didnt grow up good but was all right as a child till he woke up one day old and strange. Dang, yo. Look at that. Barenaked Ladies put real ass emotions to musical song.

One things for sure. Midgets not gonna see her brother crying anymore like a pussy. I take the whole table a candies, not including the apples cuz Dag was right that idea was idiotical, and pour them in a bag thats clean except how I just pulled Robbies dirty laundry out, and once the candies are mixed even I cant tell whats razor bladed or sharp glassed or drugged or chemicaled or what. I give the bag to Midge for holding and I go out the front door and take a long breath that goes down cold as supermilk.

Only instead of things going nice and chill things focus up sharp. Theres no fumes out here. No steam from Robbies shower either. I count five or six or seven trick or treaters carrying bags down the way. Ones a Batman, ones a Transformer, and ones a Little Pony. One I notice special cuz shes hauling ass for Robbies place like shes got a magical hunch weve got the goods.

If that girls our first treater, I dont want to see her face, all right? Not yet, okay? Id prefer about anything else to look at so I check my sneaks and sitting right there is that shriveled ass jackolantern nobody had the decency to chuck. Its how Midget left it with duck tape over the holes to keep her pumpkin bug friends locked inside. But the air out here has me thinking clear. What the hells little sister doing? If youve got friends, you cant be sealing them up. You got to let them escape your sorry ass pumpkin world.

I lift my snowboot and smash. Orange guts go blasting. I stomp till its flat and bugs are scrambling off like theyre lifted. Theyre free now to live their stupid bug lives and it was the right thing to do but that doesnt mean Im not sad. Moms bought this pumpkin for me and now that its squashed it reminds me a Moms worse than ever. Am I even gonna see Moms and her bedsore ass after tonight? No, Jody, dont think on that. You think on that too long and you end up in a room without any color except the beautiful papers your best bitch mails you.

The trick or treat girls clopping up the walk now. Theres no dodge to be had. This is my thing now. I own it. I whisper to myself the best bull I can and it comes out like a prayer, like Dick Trickle got his God stuff stuffed inside my brain. Prayer goes something like how each a the children thatll be swallowing our candies has a soul, right? Maybe I can catch them souls to plug up the holes I have inside me that normal kids dont have. And maybe thats some selfish ass behavior. But who knows whats right or wrong when it come to souls. No way it can be good letting them go to waste.

Doesnt matter much in the end cuz when I get brave enough to look I see the girl isnt no trick or treater anyhow. This shorty here I recognize easy as pie even though shes sporting a costume that cant hardly even be believed.

The Fly

It happens all the time in movies. Some boys tuxedoed up and waiting to take his ho to prom and all of a sudden she shows up at the top a the stairs so banging the camera has to slow way down so we can appreciate the dress and the shoes and the hair and the face and the tits and the booty and everything. Its a super magical moment.

Thats how it goes with Dag. No fooling. She stops right in front a Robbies door and even though her face is painted up silver I can tell shes going slow motion to see if I think shes beautiful. Theres no fronting required on that. My fool heads nodding. Just nodding and nodding cuz I never saw anything so beautiful in my whole life. She smiles and my heads about to pop clean off cuz it reminds me how Dags the whole package, beautiful for sure, Id hit that no doubt, but also full a intellect and imaginative and helpful and talented. Shes a clever bitch too cuz her secret ass costume is nothing like I guessed. No princess, no fairy, none a that predictable boring ass business.

Shes done herself up like a fly. Fly arms and fly wings and fly eyes and the whole thing so sparkly it hurts to look. But think on it. Thats how flies are. They sparkle in the sun same as ticks sparkle on a dog with the main difference that flies dont suck blood, theyre flying free. This outft isnt something Dags folks bought at no store. Girlfriend invented this all by her dang self.

Shortys got six arms. Two real arms plus four skinny fly arms. When I look close I spot the tiny yellow numbers that inform me its pipe insulation. The reason I know about pipe insulation is one time Robbie purchased a bunch. I dont know why. To insulate some pipes, I guess? Fat boy never insulated nothing though so me and Midget devised famous swords from Middle Earth. Pipe insulation makes sweet ass swords but let me promise you a fact. It makes fly arms even better.

On Dags head shes sporting big fly eyes built out a what looks like styrofoam plus ten tons a red glitter. Glitter all over her outfit too and her shoes as well and also the ground. For real, theres a whole trail of glitter from where she came from and thats the most magical thing of all cuz Yellow Streets the most ugly ass street you ever knew but now its glittering. Come morning, that glitter will be gone down the sewer but tonight? Tonight Dag did something special for all our asses.

Dag does a slow twirl. On her back shes attached fly wings and theyre as gorgeous as any stuff made in the history of stuff. Its so gorgeous I choke like a chump. Theyre sculptured out a wire but Dag bent it all intricate so it has designs like maple leafs and ocean waves and fiery flames. Stretched across the wire is something thin and glisteny like saran wrap and when the breeze blows it flutters like the most delicate thing.

The wings are attached with beautiful bows to a black leotard so tight you can see through it to Dags bod, except Dag markered the leotard in silver all strategic so you cant peep no nips or bush. Mostly she markered spirals. Spiral tits, spiral shoulders, spiral elbows, spiral bellybutton, spiral knees, spiral booty, and between the spirals she markered even smaller spirals so if you search too hard for nudity you just get dizzy. Trust me on this!

Dag lifts up her natural arms and her four fake arms come up too cuz theyre connected with strings. It takes me a sec cuz Im a dumb ass, but I realize shes saying come get a hug. That touches my heart and whatnot cuz I havent been feeling the love from Dag since that rough business went down with Gwendolyn.

Before I go in for the hug Im real thankful I threw my Grishnákh stuff at Robbie cuz that would a been some weak ass Halloween disguise next to this. Besides, man, I can do better than Grishnákh. Tonight Im the biggest hero of all. Im Aragorn, son of Arathorn, heir of Isildur, rightful claimant to the thrones of Arnor and Gondor, and Dags the Half Elf Arwen, youngest child of Elrond of Rivendell, the High Elves last Evenstar and granddaughter of Lady Galadriel. Sure its a shame we cant retire our asses among the Rohirrim near the forest Fangorn where we can plant junk and plow junk and drink fresh goat milk and have intercourse all over the dang farm. But theres a bigger battle and we been called to fight. Thats not a choice. Thats destiny and me and Dag are stuck in it.

The hug isnt for me though. Dag glides right by. One a my fingers touches her body or her thorax or whatever you call it and thats the best feel I can cop. I turn around and theres

Midget. Little sisters standing on the other side the screen door like she forgot what planet shes on. Eyes big as hell. Hands hanging like bricks. Hair glued up in flypaper and she dont even care a hoot.

I get it. I get it now. Dag didnt invent and design this costume for me. Didnt keep it on the DL for me either. Dag did this, all this, for Midge, she did it for little sister, and when Dag opens the door and steps her insect ass inside I follow behind cuz even though I been left out a the whole hug situation I got a feeling this might be the most important emotional moment I ever see.

Midgets the flypaper. Dags the fly. When they wrap their eight arms around each other it makes a duck tape sound cuz a how flypapers stick to pipe insulation. Dag asks Midge real soft if she knows flypaper has arsenic in it. Yo, for real? I didnt know that myself. That seems like important wisdom to know.

Dagflys exactly who Midges been waiting for since the day I first knew her foster ass and she puts her whispery mouth to Dags ear and all the secrets Midges got stored up all this time comes pouring out like dog blood, like pumpkin guts, and Dags eyes pop like shes shocked and then go sad like shes sad and then go thoughtful. I shut the door behind us and lean on it and observe the whole living room scene real respectful and listen to the musical geniuses Barenaked Ladies do their last song. Cant hear a word my girlies are whispering but thats all right. Thats all right. I feel pretty dang lucky just to be here.

Lotte,

Your fish are dead. Surprise. They've been dead the whole time. Right after Mama and Papa locked you up, they decreed the Big Flush. Morrissey, Johnny, Andy, and Mike went loop de loop until they took the big waterslide to the sewer. Mama didn't think I could care for them properly while juggling my copious activities. I cried like a little brat back then, but Mama was right. If something's destined to croak, don't let it swim around forever suffering. You're the one who said the Clinic is a fish bowl. Do you wish the docs would give you the Big Flush?

I didn't finish your last letter. I got to the part where you said you were "acutely concerned" about me, and laughed until I cried and the letter got too soggy to read, although I give you props for scrounging up flowered stationery in the Clinic. You realize that's where you live, right? And what that makes you? I have the highest grade point average in my class. I'm the president of six clubs. I'm athletic and artistic. I'm a B-cup. I'm beautiful.

I can do anything I want.

When Mrs. Rivers my dance teacher claps like a retarded

seal, I imagine she's trying to put out the fire I set to her dress. When Mr. Homewood the gymnastics coach tells me to run the routine again, I imagine doing it naked like I know he wants, so I can watch him cry in shame over his boner. When Ms. Tubb my Quiz Bowl coach says, "What's the capital of Botswana?" I say "Gaborone," but what I hear from my mouth is, "How much wine do you have to drink, Ms. Tubb, to live with being this pathetic?"

Wow, am I looking forward to not pretending anymore.

The same thing happened to Robbie. People dumped praise on him for insignificant achievements until he got drunk on it. Gee, he carried a brown ball over an arbitrary line of paint?! You should see this scrapbook Robbie has. It's loaded with articles drooling over how astounding he was. Where's all those reporters now? Slobbering all over some new boy carrying a new ball, that's where.

Letting Robbie believe he was somebody ruined his life. I won't let it ruin mine. My scrapbook's like a tick about to pop. It's three times the size of Robbie's, which means it's three times as hazardous. Lotte, let's not forget your scrapbook was a big juicy tick too before Mama mysteriously "misplaced it," and hmmm, how did life work out for you, ha ha ha?

One day Jody wondered if his mom kept a scrapbook of him, and I asked if he'd ever done anything worth putting in a book. He looked sad, but really he should be proud. Realizing your "accomplishments" are fake is what growing up feels like. The pitiful thing is most people never realize it. The only non-fake thing you ever did, Lotte, the only thing you ever did for you, was try to kill yourself. You did a crummy job of it, but I respect you gave it the old college try.

I'm not going to pussy out like you did. They're going to need a lot more than one stomach pump to fix what we're going to do. Remember in my first letter I said I didn't have any dark secrets? I sure do now. Robbie had an idea that's going to educate this town on how you don't mess up kids and expect they won't mess you up back. I think Robbie was joking when he came up with it, but it felt like my skin caught on fire. He'd have dropped it, but I kept bringing it back up. I encouraged him, complimented him. Pretty soon it wasn't a joke, and best of all, Robbie believed he'd planned the whole thing himself without any help from anyone, which, as you know, is critical when you're dealing with males.

What would you think if you looked down your sweet little sister's throat and all you saw were miles of rusty pipe? Is that a strange thing to ask? I have thoughts like this all the time and never tell anyone, not even Jody. My heart is a crow with oily black feathers. Does it take a crazy person like you to make sense of a crazy thing like that? My eyeballs are filled with dog fangs. Did your eyes ever feel like they could bite?

When you do hear what we did, you won't approve. I daresay you'll be "acutely concerned." Watch out, Lotte! Those doctors are turning you back into the robot girl you used to be. The robot girl I pretend to be. I hope one day, when we're both locked up in different places, you'll think of what I did, and why I did it, and who I am, and I hope truly and sincerely that you'll feel pride.

If you don't, well, whatever. I absorbed you a long time ago, just like The Glenn will absorb Yellow Street, just like "The Blob." Remember that movie? It was a whole lot better than "Deadgirl," "Antichrist," and "Martyrs," which I did watch but only made me feel sorry for you. Those movies are no fun at all. I have fun all the time. Don't you wish you were me, ha ha ha?

The only thing not fun is writing this letter. Sorry, just being honest. Writing you is boooooooring. I guess I do it out of habit. Everyone does pointless things out of habit. Jody keeps trying to make his mom better. Robbie keeps reliving his past. The only habit Midge has is sticking with Jody, and Jody's all right, but he's not the role model she needs.

That's why I'm going to try to bond with Midget before it happens, girl-to-girl. She's just the right size to be my new Clara Bear McGrumpy, ha ha ha. I love Midget. She's the only person I've ever known who's never hurt anyone. You think it's because she doesn't talk? Maybe once you start talking in life, all the rotten evil way down safe inside you (example: the things I'd like to do to Mrs. Rivers, Mr. Homewood, and Ms. Tubb) begins leaking from your mouth like second-hand smoke and soon everyone around you gets cancer.

I was your little sister, Lotte, and I liked it for a while. I really did. But I'm the older sister now, and I'm going to be a better one than you. That's a bitchy thing to say, but that's what I love about Jody and the gang. Everyone in the world is awful, including Mama, Papa, you, and me. The difference is, over on Yellow Street you don't have to hide it.

Happy Halloween.
Dag

My Wiener Part 3: The Return of the King

Size a my wiener isnt gonna trouble me any more cuz things arent all about busting your nut. Whyd it take me so long to figure that out? Even in porn, the sex stuff doesnt last that long, not really, not when you compare it to a whole life. Whats important is that me and Dag and Midget are fam. Dag is the moms and Im the pops and Midges the child and the three of us, what we should do when Halloweens done is go live together, help each other out and be kind to each other and whatnot, and if Dag and me have sexual relations, well thats all right with me but Im not gonna be pressuring her. If she wants, maybe we can have some babies so Midge can learn to play normal, this time with some nice ass children. Maybe we give them all bug names so she feels comfortable. Beetle and Bumblebee and Cricket and Firefly. Have us a whole swarm a kids, invent us up some love with nothing more than her puss and my wiener. Cuz why not? Answer me that, you think youre so smart. We invent us up some love. Sure we do. Why the hell not.

Mrs F

Doorbell dings super loud right under me and I jump off the door like its electrified. Me and Midget rung that bell a hundred times this afternoon and Im telling you it never made that wild animal screech. I behave like a piss pants bitch and look for Robbie like hes the Ranger sent to save my Hobbity ass. Fat boy comes out a the bathroom pimped like a player, hair slick, shirt tucked, looking pro except for the toilet paper spots all over his face. Robbie checks Dag and Midget, and Dag and Midget check me, and I check Robbie, and Robbie checks us, and I know what thought is firing simultaneous in all our heads.

<Go away.> Thats what our asses are thinking. <We are not ready.>

And it goes quiet. And that quiet is tense.

Doorbell dings again. This time it sounds like a siren. Theres a tornado coming, take cover. Third time it dings its too late, the tornados crashing up Yellow Street to smoosh us flat. Situation in the crib is panicked and Robbie has his blubber belly in his hands like hes fixing to diarrhea his guts out again, but no, not this time, hes the mature ass adult here and he knows hes got to step up, balls out, chrome up, and roll hard.

Robbie wheezes a noisy breath and tightens his tie like hes got a presentation to make at the office and acts fast before he can think twice. He lets go a his tummy and snatches up the dangerous candy bag and hurries by so speedy I take a elbow on the head and it stings. Up close Robbie dont look so pimp. His skins runny like wax and hes got shaving cream in his ears and theres damp spots all across his dope ass button shirt. First time Robbie grabs the knob his hand slips right off cuz the sweat. He has to calm down before he grabs it good.

Two tiny children in costumes. Hardly a surprise, right? So how come my hearts going so hard? Outfits arent superior like Dags but theyre easy to guess. Ones a rabbit cuz she has rabbit ears and the others a raccoon cuz she has black gunk around her eyes. Both a them are blond white girls with expensive costumes and that right theres a red colored flag cuz they sure as hell arent from Yellow Street and thats got me alarmed till I focus on their adult. I know this bitch. I know this nice old bitch with the round glasses and the brown and gray hair thats mostly gray now. Bitch is none other than Mrs Fullerton.

When Mrs F smiles shes got brown old people teeth. She gives a little pat to Rabbit and Raccoon and they go <Trick or treat>. It sounds weak though cuz theyre nervous about big huge Robbie looming tall like a chainsaw psycho and also the whole hood in general with all the broke glass and jimmy hats and drug baggies not to mention the hood rats giggling scary in the dark. Rabbit and Raccoon dont belong here. Theyre not dumb.

Mrs F laughs real good though just like Mrs F always does. Kind a laugh that makes a young killer wonder if shes gonna gift his ass a delicious strawberry pie. Im glad as hell to see the dried up old uppity up before I realize just what exactlys going down.

Rabbit and Raccoon are holding out their plastic pumpkin baskets for treats. Robbies standing there holding the bag full a dangerous candies. And Mrs Fs getting her a funny look cuz isnt nobody budging.

Old lady touches the top a her jugs like she forgot her manners. She goes <Robbie, dear, these are my granddaughters> and she taps their animal heads with her finger that has a big gold ring on it and says both their names. Real nice little white girl names no doubt but they dont make it to my brain cuz Im shook. Mrs F? Mrs Fs granddaughters? Hows this all happening? Mrs F goes <Arent they adorable?> and Robbie doesnt move and she goes <They are the lights of my life, these two pests> and Robbie doesnt move and she goes <Ive missed having little children around> and Robbie doesnt move.

Rabbit and Raccoons plastic pumpkins droop cuz theyre confused. Mrs F covers it up good though cuz one thing Mrs Fs skilled at is talking. She goes <These are Roys children, dear. I dont get to see them enough these days, not nearly enough for a pinchy fingered old woman like myself. Remember I told you Roy and his family moved to Virginia? Seems like yesterday, I know, but its been four years now. Of course I

cant blame him, Merck made him a wonderful offer and you dont get offers like that every day. Its good for the children. Safe neighborhood, good schools. But Id be lying if I said it doesnt make a grandmother lonely.>

Robbies lips are moving. Just a little. If we were wagering Id wager hes trying to say <Yes, maam> just like he always says to Mrs F except right now fat boy cant make a peep.

Mrs F says <Roy and his wife are at a dinner party tonight with some of his old friends. They were going to skip it so these munchkins could have their trick or treating but I said, no, no, you two go ahead and have fun with your friends. Just leave old Nana the candy gathering duties, me and my sore knees will survive. Of course, I dont mind at all. I think its a gas. Everyone seems to have more fun when theyre wearing masks, dont they? And that includes the adults! Well, now Im prattling.>

A ball a sweats hanging suspenseful to Robbies nose and it alerts me how Im sweating too, bad sweat like Im pissing out through my skin all the ill junk Ive done. Dang. Howd I do so much ill junk in one day? I stole and lied and cussed and disrespected elders and killed a dog and did unnatural stuff with chemicals. When that evil business leaves your body it produces a cloud a odor. Thats evolution right there. You stink so bad you got to move your ass if you want out a the cloud.

<When we spoke on the phone earlier.> This is Mrs F talking. <That wasnt like you, dear. You were so short with me. Im an old lady without much to do so Ive been dwelling on it all day.

And the conclusion I came to was that you havent sounded happy in a long time. In fact, I think its been getting worse. Am I imagining it? Oh, I know its no business of mine. I know I can be a busybody. Believe me, I hear it from Roy all the time. Perhaps Ive doted on you for too long. Youre not a child, of course, you can take care of yourself. If you feel Ive overstepped my boundaries here, feel free to tell me off. Go ahead, give me a piece of your mind. It wouldnt be the first time I hear it and wont be the last, I can promise you that.>

This lady. This old white lady here. That visits Yellow Street in the dark like it isnt a thing. That talks to Robbie like hes not fat and pimply. Like he doesnt sweat gross. Like hes not a freak the whole town hopes just crawls off and dies. Is something broke with her little round glasses? Has her brain alzheimered? Man, I dont know, but next thing the crazy old nice bitch does is put her knuckly old lady hand around Robbies bicep.

Whys she got to touch him and make things humiliating? How many times did Robbie use his pullup bar to muscle out some a that flab? It didnt work. Isnt ever gonna work either. Robbies gonna be fat dumb Robbie forever. All a us gonna be all a us forever. No old lady no matter how friendly she is has special powers to change none a those unfortunate facts. Mrs F digs in her claws, though, and she tries. Dang if she doesnt try good.

<People around here give you a raw deal for what you did to that coach. It wasnt fair then and its not fair now. I am positive, in my heart, that you had your reasons. I dont even need to

know what those reasons were. You are not a violent person, Robbie. You just feel things very deeply.>

Mrs F moves her hand to where Robbies neck lards fatted out over his pimp collar. Mrs F blinks and blinks and her eyes are shining.

<You saved my Roy. You saved my Roy when no one else was brave enough to do it. These girls here? My granddaughters? My granddaughters whom I love so dearly? They would not be here if not for you. You remember that. You look at them standing here, in the flesh, and you be proud of that. I wish Roy would have come with us tonight. I asked him to but you know how it is. He doesnt even remember that night. He knows he has that scar on his neck but beyond that it doesnt mean much to him. I love that son of mine, but hes wrong. It means a great deal. Hes at that dinner party tonight, with his wife, with his friends, because of your courage. Remember that when times are tough. And theyre tough now, I can see that. Courage like yours does not disappear with age.>

Robbies head tilts down like he cant look at any old persons face anymore. He looks at Rabbit and Raccoon and he looks at their plastic pumpkins and he looks at his bag a evil candies and he looks at the floor. Mrs F scratches the back a his greasy hair the same as how me and Dag scratched Gwendolyn before we sent her to doggie heaven and then Mrs F takes her hand back and it lands right between Rabbits rabbit ears. I think up a joke to crack cuz jokes are what Im skilled at and jokes help lighten the mood, and it goes something like how Ive never seen a rabbit or raccoon on Yellow Street that wasnt roadkilled. Its funny up in my head but it wont drag its jokey ass across my tongue.

<Now.> Mrs F straights up her back like shes school teaching. <If its all right with you Im going to ignore what you said on the phone and Im going to continue calling you at the end of each month the same as Ive always done. Furthermore, this Nana here plans to keep calling you until the day they turn off my life support. Is that understood?>

Robbie nods. He doesnt look at her but he nods.

She goes <Well, now, I see you have some young guests. Hello, Jody, its very nice to see you again. Hello, friends of Jodys.>

<Hello, maam> I say.

<Hello, maam> Dag says.

Midget doesnt talk.

<And I also see you have yourself a big bag of candy. We cant let that go to waste, can we, girls? Youve got a big night ahead of you, Robbie, and we shall not take up any more of your time.>

Mrs F. Such a nice old uppity up. At least Ive always figured she was nice. Now Im thinking of all the folks on Yellow Street, or in the whole town, or in the whole world that screwed up but dont have a nice bitch to forgive them cuz theyre not pitiful enough like Robbie and no ones giving them a second and third and fourth and hundredth chance like Mrs F does. Maybe none of its got sharkweek to do with Robbie. Maybe Mrs F does it to make herself feel better about being a rich old white bitch.

I got lots of questions but then Mrs F does the worst thing she could ever do. She pokes her bony knuckles into Rabbit and Raccoon and they do like good girls and lift up their plastic pumpkins. Theyre shy, you know? But their shy ass smiles are the genuine article cuz kids are kids no matter what hood they come from, and kids crave candies even if they come from a laundry bag of a big scary dude on Yellow Street.

Robbie peeks in the bag. Its deep and dark inside and he cant see nothing but I know for a fact how it smells. Smells like beer bottle and bug spray and bleach and metal but also chocolate and cherry and sour apple and grape. Robbie holds the bag right under his fat chin and breathes it in real slow. Look, man. You can tell yourself whatever bull you want. You can pretend how later on youre gonna break inside Rabbit and Raccoons bedroom and pick out the bad candies so no grief comes to Mrs F or her kin. But thats fictional lies. Once you drop those candies into those plastic pumpkins, nobodys ever gonna know what candies came from where. Gonna get all mixed up inside those little girl bellies.

Dont even mean to but I start moving. I dont know what Im planning, but somethings got to happen and its got to happen now cuz in my mind I see a video of Midget seizuring in the tub that one day after supermilk and I cant put it on pause. I reach for the laundry bag but somebodys holding me by my jean jacket. Got to be Dag, right? Six fly legs make her hold six times stronger. Or maybe its Midget, you know? Maybe her flypaper outfit flypapered my jacket and I got stuck. Or maybe its not either of my bitches. Maybe I just come to my senses cuz dang. This isnt my story to end. This is Robbies story. End a the day, its his play to make, not mine.

Robbie puffs his cheeks like hes still gots puke to puke and his teeth rattle around like a bunch a loose marbles and stink drops squeeze out a his skin so thick they fall like rocks. He does it slow. He reaches out with that stank ass old laundry bag and Rabbit and Raccoons smiles are sparkling big and white, and there it goes, there goes the whole world in one second, that bag dipping low and them plastic pumpkins rising high and theres no going back, theres no bus pass thats gonna bus us back from this place Robbie took us.

The fist holding the laundry bag changes path. It grabs the knob. Little girls faces go dumb like what? Mrs Fs face goes surprised like what? Its painful and hurtful cuz theres some serious relationship things going down with Robbie and Mrs F. At the same time though the hurt punches quick like a needle and then its over, Robbie shuts the door right in their friendly ass faces and the whole things over, and to me it feels like we all cried real hard just once at the same exact time except havent none a us made a single pipsqueak mouse or bug or man or little ass child sound.

Ghosts

We stare at the door like its our job till we half hear Mrs F speaking some words to her grandkids and the whole group a them shuffles their candyless asses off the stoop. We keep staring. For real, like its our jobs. Car doors open, check. Car doors shut, check. Engine revs up quick like its a new ride, check. After that, I dont know. None of us can say. I guess Mrs F and her crew goes back to a hood where they can beg themself top junk like gold foil candies with french words and salt.

Robbie droops. Thats the only way to put it. His neck goes like rubber. His flab cheeks and lips go like baloney. Even his tits sag under his button shirt. Last thing that happens is his fingers go loose and the laundry bag falls to the floor and it crunches and crackles like its full a dead bugs.

Earlier when Dag socked the light switch? Thats nothing. No way Dag ever acted in the history of Dag compares to this explosion. Her eyes turn to the kind a glass balls they put at the bottom of fish tanks and her face goes neon pink like its melting off her dang skull and her jaw is like the screws melted off, it opens huge and salivas bubbling inside like too hot soup and she screams and all I want to do is fall on the floor and cover Midge cuz its the loudest worst thing I ever heard in my life.

<<<They treated you like garbage, Robbie! You've crawled on your belly for ten years for a bunch of worthless snakes who dont care about anything or anyone except their perfect homes and perfect children! You didnt hurt them at all compared to how they hurt you! Theyre supposed to pay, Robbie!>>>

Robbie holds his head like Dags words are every linebacker he ever footballed against concussioning him one after the other.

Dags spit is like blood. <<<They have to pay and this is the night they have to do it! You planned it! We planned it! Your stupid scrapbook hasnt had a new story in a million years but that was going to change tonight! All our stupid scrapbooks would finally have something worth putting in them! You cant puss out now, Robbie! I wont allow it!>>>

Robbie slaps her. I never saw any part of Robbie move so fast. Its like his hands a separate animal. Like #69 Kyle Ketchums ferret in a scarf. It cracks Dags good and her pink cheek goes purple and I can see the outline of Robbies fingers and even the palm lines that look like the squiggly roads at Pinebluff Glenn Estates. The slap echoes like all a us are in a majestic canyon except no one feels inspired. I dont think none a us feel nothing but numb.

In all my days I never saw a man move so sad. Robbies slapping arm floats around underwater style. Real slow he turns and starts sliding his feet across the carpet. Just like the dozers they scoop a path straight through the trash he built up his whole adult ass life. He doesnt look up once. Its like hes not even living. Like hes a dead body trying to find its grave. It takes a million minutes for fat boy to get to his bedroom and the last thing he does before he makes it is grab his bottle a Mad Dog. No last words, nothing. He shuts the door and hes gone. You can hear the springs in the bed go zing but nothing after that.

Dags holding her purple cheek. Her wings are quivering bad and theyre so precious and delicate Im worried theyre gonna rip. She foots the bag a candies like its a dog and shes checking if the dog is sleeping or dead or what. I guess its dead though cuz girlfriend ends up kicking it till candies go flying like guts. Shortys been emotional today and shes been hard too but this mood here is different from both. This is mean. After a time she tires her ass out and wanders a figure eight. Her glittery shoe kicks a McDonald bag and it goes up like a balloon.

Fly parts crinkle loud when she bends over. Where the McDonald bag was she finds my dragon throwing disc with the grim reaper scythes. She gives that stainless steel beauty a careful close inspection. Nobodys ever held my ninja stars but me. I dont know, it weirds me out. I have to admit, though, Dag holds it proper like shes been taking ninja lessons on the sly longside her piano and tap and flute. The big difference is her folks didnt choose this particular skill. Dag chose it herself.

She scratches Gwendolyns dry blood off the dragon like shes pondering the true meaning of that tragic event. Meantime Im criticizing my punk ass cuz I shoulda scraped off that blood myself. Or scrubbed it in the back a Robbies toilet.

Or chucked the whole lethal weapon down the dang sewer instead of just dropping it careless on Robbies floor. Then if Dag wanted a sharp deadly object shed have to go select a Ginsu knife.

Dag throws me and Midget a look and it blinds me so bad I wish I had Barack Obama to hide in. Girlfriends red glitter fly eyes are bright as hell. Her human eyes are glittering too. Its like shes a wolf. Like shes a ocean. Like shes fire. No loser ass behavioral problem crybaby like mes got any business getting in the way a that wild bright light.

She tucks the dragon disc in her right hand and with her left hand reaches out. I start sweating. Its almost November, right? And the heat company shut off Robbies service forever ago, right? Still my sweat comes bubbling. But this is the second time I mistaked the same thing. Its not me Dags reaching for. Dags holding her hand out for Midge. Half a me feels relief so much I think Im gonna cry. Crying is all my bitch ass does anymore anyway. Other half a me feels mournful though cuz little sister is my sister and if its come to this, I guess I failed being a brother.

Midgets excited like a pup. Cant lie and say shes not. She takes Dags hand and both a them look happy. I cant blame them. Midget had me and Moms for a spell but we didnt do her any favors. Dag had herself a sister for a spell too but that sisters long gone. Its Midges turn to flypaper her ass to a different fly. For a sec the new pair a sisters look at me and theres no mistaking it, not even if youre a fool like me. Its a offer to join up with their new fam even though they know I dont belong. Irregardless its a nice offer. All I got to do is jump my ass in there and crack wise and be good old Jody like I always been. Sure, Midge might a took Dags hand first but Dags a insect now and shes got lots a extra hands for holding on to if holding ons what you mean to do. I guess it isnt though cuz I dont move.

Dag and Midget cross the room graceful. Both a them step so gentle their feet dont crunch on anything. Its like theyre flying instead a walking. Flying like actual flies. Its beautiful as hell but I want to yell at them to stop. Midget enjoys standing on her head, right? How about I order her to do it right now? Stop flying, turn this whole situation upside down. But nothing I say now is going to change a thing, not for Robbie. He promised Dag a big ass event tonight and one way or the other hes gonna deliver it.

Dag opens Robbies door super quiet and peeks in smiley and mischievous. I know Dag though. Under that purple slapped cheek shes never looked more full a wrath. The two a them tiptoe inside silent. Only mistake they make is how the dragon disc scrapes a big long scrape in Robbies door. Robbie, though, he doesnt groan or snore or sniffle or nothing. I guess hes asleep or drunk or just doesnt care what happens next.

Door shuts soft. Im by my lonesome. No, man. This isnt how Halloweens supposed to go. I cant just stand here looking at a big long scrape on a door and hearing girlie whispers about how you need to rid yourself a ticks before they drain you out. Lucky for me theres new noises to think about. Little children. A big bunch a children. Theyre at the door. Dang, theyre straight up begging for treats.

Cribs so dark it makes hearing easy. The moods getting prickly out there and children are bottlenecking, a whole herd chanting for candies. The doorbell rings once and that sets off more ringing and more ringing cuz ringing doorbells is fun as hell, everybody knows that. Noise gets louder and louder but none of it fusses me. Its funny if you think about it. Some crazy sharkweek can happen in a single day, huh? Makes a robocop think. Look at me now. Im alone. Im in charge. Im the adult. Man, how the hell did that happen?

Dag kicked the laundry bag good but its still got weight. Lot less heavy than Gwendolyn and I took care a that business just fine, didnt I? Dont ask me why but picking up the bag gets me ruminating on #69 Kyle Ketchum. That rude assbutt told Robbie how he didnt have any good options in life after Coach S got disfigured. But thats not true. Theres lots a options out there for a killer. You just got to learn to visualize.

Take me for example. I could escape out the back a the crib and weave my ass through the junk and chuck the candy bag in the woods and clean the blood under my nails and make like none a this ever happened. Thats one option. Option two is I sit my ass down and feast on these dangerous candies myself. Im hungry, man. Havent ate all day. No supermilk, no McDonald, not even one a them wack ass apples. What if I choose real careful? What if I feel the candies for sharp items and sniff out the chemicals? My abs are strong as hell cuz the Oblique Side Bend and Rock n Roll Core and Half Seated Leg Circle. Maybe my abs are stronger than poison. Maybe my abs can squeeze drugs into nutrients and scrunch razor blades so small Id just poop them out like pennies.

Option three? Option three is I be a grown ass adult. Option three is I go open the door and be like <Happy Halloween> to the children and see what Im made of when rough junk starts to go down. Rough junk like a uniform taking away Midget and fostering her off to some cold blooded foster parental. Thats a hard option cuz lets be real. The fosters in this town are crooked. I learned that with DAndre. And if a town cant take care of a single nice quiet little girl doesnt that mean that town deserves what it gets?

Of all the days to revenge his personal history Robbie picked Halloween. Never thought on it till now but Robbie picked wise. Christmas and Thanksgiving and July Four are all about family and Robbie didnt have family left besides us. Halloween, though? Halloweens the one holiday bigger than family. Its about the whole community. You go out, you knock on doors you dont knock on normally, and you trust your neighbors with your tiny defenseless children. I can see how that might be inspirational. Might be. Unless you live in this hood thats being ate alive by dozers and no trust hasnt been ever earned by nobody.

This is the Return of the King right here. This is Mount Doom. Im feeling my boy Frodo, feeling him deep. Its difficult as hell to take the only power you ever had and plunk it in the lava, even if that power is some evil ass stuff.

I open the door. I do it cuz its Halloween and opening doors is what you do. Maybe its cuz my pinkeyes blurry but I cant tell if theres two children out there or two hundred demanding candies. All I know is they got bright cat eyes and faces white like sugar cuz theyre all dressed up like budget ass ghosts. They must think Im the new Robbie. Am I? Do I got impressive Irish king or Robert E Lee blood in me too? I cant think straight about it. Im not sure Ill ever think straight about nothing ever again.

Then comes a miracle from the ghost of Midget past. One of Robbies clocks goes off. All right. Nothing strange about that. Then another clock goes. Then another clock after that. Pretty quick the whole house is clocking, ding dong and bing bong. You heard what I said before. Each of them clocks are keeping different times. So what does it matter if I hand out candies or not? Nows not now anymore, you feel me? Nobody tonight is getting done in by drugs stuck in Pumpkin Peeps or sharp objects hid inside Three Musketeer. Just listen. Listen to the clocks. All that awful stuff either happened way back in the past or way off in the future.

But next thing I know Im moving. I know them clocks are omens but bad or good omens I dont know. A couple ghost kids try to ghost grab the candy bag but Im too wily and real quick Im past the pumpkin guts and down the steps. I go around the house corner and stop under Robbies bedroom window, panting bad cuz my lungs are killing me like I just did a gym mile instead a twenty feet. Maybe its cuz I know what I got to do. I got to bury these candies. Like Robbie buried his tarantulas. Like everyone buries all the things that bring them shame.

Thats when right in front of my face I find a man stone cold standing. Hes popping the scariest mask I ever saw except its no mask. Its a real life face. But a face that got grinded hard in Robbies supermilk blender. The nose looks like it got dissected and all the pieces taken out for science. One eye is staring up crazy at the moon. The skins got gobs a red and brown worms under it that arent actually worms, theyre the crookedest puffiest scars I ever saw. I know who it is all right. Its Deformo, the ugliest most frightening ass boogeyman bum that ever lived. The dozers finally chased his ass right to Robbies door.

Deformos mouth opens like hes gonna make a monster noise. Half his teeth are deep revolting holes and the top jaws way over here and the bottom jaws way over there and a river a drools pouring down so heavy his sweaties black with it. Takes me a second to read the sweatie. It says <KNIGHTS>.

Check it. I know, lots a people got <KNIGHTS> sweaties. But how many are in this bad a shape? Maybe he's Deformo now but back when that sweatie was crisp he must a had a name like everybody else, a job too, and I have a feeling that job was Coach.

The mans not deformed at all. Hes disfigured and thats a different thing. I was real careful never to get too close to Deformo in the past but still dont know how I never theorized it. #69 Kyle Ketchum said Coach S lost everything the day of the Robbie beat down and right here in my grill is all thats left. Coach S turned into a thing that lives under a bridge and has a monster face and is ten times bonier than Dick Trickle because who wants to get close enough to a monster to give him a sandwich? Not me. Im standing right in front of him and I might fall down crying.

Coach S points into his spitty saliva mouth.

<Foo> he says but I know he means <Food>. He's been begging for it for ten years.

Out a the window right above my frozen ass Robbies bed goes zing zing and the Mad Dog splatters onto the floor, or something that sounds like Mad Dog. Its real ominous and I dont like it filling up my earholes. I guess Im lucky cuz it gets drowned out by all the clocks still clocking and the ghosts still laughing and still doorbelling and the dozers still coming, still coming. The whole loud mess lifts around me a ice cold ocean that soothes the itch I been feeling my whole life. The clocks are a good omen after all. No doubt.

Coach S points at the candy bag. Im crying but might be smiling too cuz I can feel tears hanging on the edge a my teeth. Halloween is supposed to taste like sugar but this tastes like salt. Coach S reaches into the bag. I let him go ahead. Coach S and Robbie have what you call unfinished business but Robbies not currently present. I dont think hes coming either. So Ill be Robbie. Just for Coach S, just this once.

He dont even unwrap the Chocolate Creeper Peeper all the way. He chews it with half the wrapper on. His drool goes brown. He points at his chomping mouth and I might be grinning and I hand him a Strawberry Scary Jelly. His drool goes pink. Even though hes still gumming he points to his mouth again and I start to unwrap a Three Musketeer before he nabs it and pops it in. His drool goes red. I might be crying but Im for sure now definitely laughing and I realize I sound like all them child ghosts behind me howling in the night with throats like a thousand clocks.

See? Thats proof all this is happening way off in the future. These kids here are gonna die of old age long after the dozers finish dozing, and tonight their ghosts are just coming back to visit. They rush in fast around me and Coach S and also Robbie and Dag and Midge up in the window. I cant see no moving feet. Theyre fluttering ghost sheets and reaching ghost hands and wailing like theyre in pain but enjoying it too. They dont want candy. They want us. Theyre a fam bigger than any a us ever had, and they got space for us to join.

Sure, Ill join. Im not scared a pinch. This is the future. In the future Im no poopypants baby. Im a man. Trust me, things come out real good for all our asses. We survive that shit. We do. We have no choice.

Believe, yo.

Local Footballer Shows Promise

Freshman running back Robbie Glinton is the *Gazette* Athlete of the Week for his performance on November 18 at home versus Mount Vernon where he ran for 174 yards and scored 4 rushing touchdowns. "He has raw talent for fundamentals, a real enthusiasm for the sport, and responds well to coaching," praised a smiling Coach Jim Sorley. "We expect great things from him in the future."

THE
END

Thanks to Richard Abate, Megan Abbott, Charles Ardai, Andrew Karre, Amanda Kraus, Paul Mann, Maryse Meijer, Javier Ramirez, Grant Rosenberg, Julia Smith, and Onur Tukel.